B IS FOR BOWIE

ASSASSINZ ROMANTIC THRILLERS

E.L. SNOW

ASSASSINZ
ROMANTIC THRILLERS

". . . these *craftsmen* have come to terrify them, to throw down the horns of the nations who have lifted up *their* horns against the land of Judah in order to scatter it."

— ZECHARIAH 1:18-21

I am in a bad place at a bad time.

Make that the worst place at the worst time.

But how could I have known? Nobody murders someone in a house of G-d until they do, and I'm there to see it.

* * *

Thud, thud, thud. The footsteps are getting louder, which means they're getting closer.

Finally, a priest I can talk to. Ask my question. Hopefully get the answer I need and head back home where I'll try to convince my parents that everything they think is true is truly false.

I rub my eyes as the space around me organizes into shapes. It's a pretty church, way prettier than its fortress-like exterior suggests. Decorative columns stretch toward the ceiling where they form intricate arches, and the honey-colored wood pews have been buffed to a high gloss. Lit candles wink from the altar, coating everything with a flickering beauty.

At the altar, a priest taps the sign of the cross against his black shirt. I take a deep breath as I smooth out the wrinkles from my long-sleeved blazer and matching mid-length skirt.

Normally I hate these clothes that make me look like I'm a frump from the 1940s. Now I hope they fulfill their intended purpose, which is to make me appear modest and serious. I give my skirt one last tug, so I don't look like someone who's been sleeping in a church even though that's exactly what I'd been doing.

My hands freeze. A man in a gray hoodie stalks out of the shadows around the nave.

I sigh—just my luck. I'm not the only person who wants a word with the priest. I sink into the pew, resigning myself to wait a few more minutes.

But then my eyes widen. Hoodie man is grasping a knife with a point that glitters in the candlelight. As he gets closer, he hoists it into the air.

The priest—his head bent, his prayers loud—doesn't see or hear the man approach.

I try to scream something, anything, but every word I know has fled. Instead, I stay still, my muscles stiff and frozen. I want to run, but where to? It's a church. Everything is out in the open.

So I stay where I am as time slams on the brakes. Although it hasn't happened yet, I anticipate what's going to happen.

And it does—in excruciatingly slow motion.

Hoodie man reaches the priest, yanks his head back, and plunges the knife into his black-shirted chest. The blade slips through the flesh and bone like a pin through silk.

The priest's eyes pop in terror and understanding. He stumbles to his feet and takes a few halting steps as blood streams down his body.

My stomach heaves.

There is so much blood.

It pools around his feet and gushes in a river behind him, turning everything red, red, red.

Hoodie man laughs as he yanks his knife out. "I hope hell is as hot as they say it is."

As if bored with the whole thing, he pulls a handkerchief from his pocket and wipes the blade clean with casual motions.

In response, my body starts to shake, each rattle down my spine tossing me from side to side, like a ship in a storm.

The priest gapes at the hoodie man. His hands clutch his heart as he tries to staunch the blood. It, though, keeps pouring through his fingers.

"You thought you were going to get away with it. That you could wait until after you were dead to pay the price." He shakes his now-unstained knife in the priest's face. "But vengeance came early."

The priest crumples to the floor.

Crack.

His head strikes the hard, unyielding marble where he twitches for a moment before falling still. His face glows an eerie white in the dancing candlelight, and his eyes have a curious, unseeing look to them.

He is dead.

All my breath has fled, and I am so cold. I rub my hands over my arms, but that does nothing to warm me up.

Hoodie man drags the priest to the altar, smearing blood behind him. He places the priest on his back, pulls his arms out to the side, and pushes his legs together into the shape of a cross.

Hoodie man yanks a sheaf of postcard-sized pictures from his jacket pocket. He peels one and places it beside the priest so that it floats on top of the lake of blood. He repeats the action until the body is looped with pictures.

I squint to get a closer look. One, another, and then all the rest come into focus. They are photos of little boys. Some have freckles; others have cowlicks; one has a pair of glasses. The similarity? They're all smiling.

"Never again will you take a little boy's smile away," he says.

Hoodie man turns, his body stiffening.

Sweat beads and then freezes on my forehead.

He has seen me.

Run, I say to my stupid, useless legs, but they refuse to move. By the time I get myself in motion, he is there, swinging an arm around me, slapping a hand over my mouth. For a moment, we stay there, not moving. Then, ever so gently, he steers me toward him until I'm pressed against his body, which is warm and solid.

He pushes me against a pew, using his body to prevent me from moving. He slides a hand to a hip and pats it before repeating the action on the other side. He's checking to see if and what I have on me.

"No phone, no weapon," he says to himself.

My heart drums against my chest, and black dots crowd my eyes. Because I don't have a cell phone, have never had one, which was never a problem until now, when it is a huge, unconquerable problem.

Breathe, Hannah, I tell myself. I don't want to faint. Because if I do, then I can't fight back. And if I don't fight back, then I might die too.

In and out.

In and out.

I do this until the black dots recede.

Hoodie man bends his head until his mouth is level to my ear. His hot breath pulses against my lobe as I tremble.

"You're coming with me," he says.

H oodie man half drags/half carries me through the bowels of the church, out the back door, and into one of those nondescript black cars that livery drivers use. He tosses me into the backseat and buckles me up before knotting my hands together with a plastic zip tie.

My heart feels like a ticking time bomb that's seconds away from exploding.

"Not a sound," he says before slamming the door.

Outside the window, a bachelorette wearing a soiled sash and lopsided tiara lurches down the street. Two women on either side support her. I frantically wave at them with my bound hands, but they don't notice. I open my mouth to scream, but hoodie man is already sliding into the front seat.

"Don't think about it," he says.

I slump into my seat as the bachelorette party disappears around the corner.

He drives us out of Manhattan and over the bridge into Queens. From dark-tinted windows, the neon and concrete of the city stream past me.

My family, I think. *They're probably finishing dinner right now.*

I dredge up an image of our last Shabbat dinner. Mom was serving various courses of challah bread, gefilte fish, and chamin—a savory stew of beef, barley, potatoes, and beans. Two candles were glimmering on the table, which represent the commandments to remember and to observe. Dad was saying said the first blessing. My four-year-old sister Salome was plucking the sleeve of her best dress, and my fourteen-year-old sister Miriam, the picture of piety, was discreetly asking Salome to stop fidgeting.

My stomach goes sour as I remember the other person who joined us, the person who is the reason I am here in this terrible jam.

My parents must be shaking with worry. I didn't tell them where I was going, sure I would be back home hours ago. Now, nobody knows where I am, and they won't have the first clue as to where they should look for me.

I clench my jaw. I should have told someone something, but I'd wanted to seize the moment, when my dad was working and my mom, in an unusual burst of energy, had stepped out with Salome and Miriam to run a few errands.

I stare out the window, trying to imprint the names of the streets in my mind. But it's so dark inside and outside of the car that I can't see anything.

I'm breathing better now, so rational thought returns, which is to say the reality of the situation hits me. I am in a car with a murderer.

I start to tremble, the violent, uncontrollable kind.

Am I going to die too, my heart sliced in half, my lifeless body thrown into the East River like a piece of garbage no one wants? Forgetting that I'd been warned not to make a sound, I cry.

These are my last moments on earth, I think as tears streak down my cheeks.

The murderer glances over his shoulder at me. The hoodie hangs low over his face, so I can't make out his features beyond a sprinkling of stubble and a strong, proud nose.

"I told you not to make a sound."

His voice is rough, and I cower in the back seat. Although my hands are bound, I have enough mobility to lift them to my eyes and press them into the corners to stop the flow. They're quivering too much to be effective, so the tears keep coming.

"I'm not going to hurt you," he says in a softer tone. "My word is my bond."

In my head, I scream, *You're a murderer. Your word counts for nothing.*

It's as if he can hear my thoughts. He sighs. "I'm not happy about this either."

We drive for a while as I struggle to control my sobs.

He looks at me again before tipping his head side to side as if he's deciding something. "Are you hungry?" he asks.

I blink at the question. *Am I hungry?*

When did I last eat? Breakfast, maybe? I seem to remember my mom pushing a piece of toasted challah into my hands, me sipping a cup of tea.

I hadn't been eating much since last week when it became official that history was going to repeat itself if I didn't do something fast.

I am hungry. The worry of the past week combined with the drama of the last hour has left me feeling as weak and famished as a new baby. But I'm not taking food from a murderer.

My stomach growls. Horrified, I clap my hands against it.

He laughs—a nice one at odds with what I know about him. "I'll take that as a yes."

Traitor, I wail to my stomach.

"I know a good mom-and-pop pizza parlor that's open all night."

Well, this is wonderful. I'm going to have dinner with a murderer.

"Plain or pepperoni?" he asks.

I don't know what to say, so I say nothing.

"I'm waiting," he says. "Or maybe I should ask your stomach."

A memory zips to the front of my mind. It's my ninth birthday, and I'm biting into a slice of sausage pizza. I'm surrounded by red balloons and my fourth-grade classmates. A stack of festively wrapped presents rests in a corner just waiting for me to open.

Say cheese, my dad says. I smile so big for the camera that my cheeks ache.

I sigh. That wasn't the last time I had sausage pizza, but it was close. Now, we follow all these rules for food, which makes pizza with meat a no-no. But if I die, is G-d going to care that my last meal is something that makes me happy?

"Sausage," I whisper.

He swings into a parking lot and pulls the car into a spot. "I'm sorry about this."

"Wha . . ."

I can't finish the word because hoodie man has ripped off a piece of duct tape and pressed it across my lips. He wraps it around my head a couple of times, going underneath my hair. It will be impossible to unravel with my bound hands.

"Precautions," he says, no joke in his voice this time. "And, just so you know, the car has fingerprinted locks. It's also tinted so dark that no one, even if they want to, can see in." He pauses. "It's not soundproof, though. And since you're going to be sitting here for a while," he points at the tape, "I had to do this."

Even with the glow from the restaurant, I still can't see his face. But his head is bowed as if he's sorry.

"You don't want more people to get hurt, do you?" He waits for my answer.

Finally, I shake my head.

"Then don't try to escape. Because if you thought things were bad earlier, they can get a whole lot worse."

I nod as I scold myself. Why didn't I let anyone know where I was going? Why didn't I run when I saw the knife in hoodie man's hands?

Why?

Why?

Why?

The word thumps in time with my terrified heart.

3

I'm sitting in hoodie man's kitchen, staring at the slice of pizza in front of me. Sausage dots the gooey white cheese, and it smells exactly the way I remember.

He got the kind I asked for. Nobody has done that in so long that I've stopped volunteering my opinion. My eyes get wet. I'm touched, which is a dumb thing to feel. It also speaks to how small my life is that someone buying me pizza makes me emotional, but that's the truth.

My mind wanders to Miriam, who's never had a birthday party with balloons and pizza. She's missed out on all the markers of childhood, her purpose fated to suit other people's agenda, just like I was at her age.

Interrupting my thoughts of the sister I have to save, he tilts his head toward my plate. "Eat. Then I'll show you around." His chin dips. "We also need to talk."

He hasn't taken off his hoodie, so his face lurks in its shadows. But now that he's seated in front of me, I can make out his build.

He's huge.

Not fat, no.

Tall, like he probably bumps his head on ceilings all the time.

Muscular, like his muscles have muscles.

Next to him, I feel small and weak, although I'm on the tall side for a woman. I'm strong, too, because my little sister Salome loves to be carried from place to place.

I touch my lips where the tape was. They're raw but not injured. I peek at hoodie man again and groan internally. Escaping is going to be a lot harder when my captor is the size of an iceberg.

My stomach grumbles.

Pizza or morals? I ask myself.

I choose pizza. I tell myself it's because I'm going to need the energy later when I escape, even though I really just want to remember if the pizza tastes as good as I remember.

For a few minutes, we sit in weirdly companionable silence, eating pizza.

"Sausage was a good choice," he says.

My cheeks warm as I look up.

He's staring at me, immobile, a slice of pizza dangling from his hand.

Out of nowhere, he says, "You look like Snow White with your black hair, pale skin, and red, red lips."

My mouth opens and closes as I entertain another potential scenario. Is he going to rape me? Is the pizza just a lure to get me to let down my guard? The slice slides out of my hand and onto the plate where it lands cheese side down.

I don't care. I'm not hungry anymore.

Hoodie man seems to guess my thought process. "I'm not going to hurt you," he says for the second time. "My word is my bond."

I laugh. I have to. He murdered someone. He one hundred percent could hurt me.

He leans toward me. "My word is my bond." His tone is low, urgent as if it's important I believe him.

I blot my lips with the napkin, avoiding his gaze. The word of a murderer is worth what, exactly?

I gaze around his kitchen. Maybe I should take mental notes, so I can describe it to the police if I escape.

When I escape, I correct myself. The pizza has perked me up, and I've committed myself to getting out of here.

The kitchen looks like a million other kitchens: white cabinets, white appliances, a white tile floor. We're sitting around a white table on white chairs. I search for any quirk or color that would make it identifiable, but I can't find anything. No pictures or magnets on the fridge, no apron with World's Best Cook stamped on it.

He reaches for my plate. "Let's move into the living room."

"Wait," I say, refusing to leave the room without a single thing that can help me. "What's your name? If your word is your bond, shouldn't I know whose bond it is?"

He rears back with a surprised laugh. "I guess you should."

"So . . ."

"Call me Bowie."

"Bowie? Is there a last name?"

He shakes his head. "Not one I'll ever tell you." He stops for a second. "Or anyone else."

"Is Bowie your real name?"

"You're smart, Snow White. It's not."

"How did you come up with Bowie?"

"It's my weapon of choice."

My jaw flops open like I'm a stupid fish. "Weapon of choice?"

Bowie reaches down and pulls out the knife he used earlier. It slips out of his fingers and clatters onto the table between our plates.

Up close, the knife is terrifying. Sharp, shiny, and curved, it has something small, almost unnoticeable, carved into the bottom of the handle. I squint until the number seventeen comes into focus. The carving is neatly done, and I suspect he did it. But why?

I zoom out and see the knife for what it is—a blade that could kill anyone with a single swipe or charge.

Will kill anyone, I correct myself. Bowie killed a priest with one thrust to the heart.

My mouth goes dry. I'm here with a murderer. Whose name is his weapon of choice.

"Some people like it for hunting, but in reality, it's a fighting knife that's similar to a snub-nosed sword." He closes his fingers around the knife's handle and stows it under his hoodie. He stands, tosses the cold pizza into the garbage, and then offers me his hand. "You'll be more comfortable in the living room."

I freeze. Is he really going to take me to the living room to talk, or is something more awful going to happen?

He continues to stand, arm extended, as the tension between us stretches like a thread about to shred.

Finally, I accept his grip, mostly because I don't know what else to do. His hand, large and warm like a mitten, closes around my cold one.

As we walk through the kitchen door, hand in hand as if we're entering a dance floor, I can't shake the image of Bowie's knife.

With my free hand, I touch the hollow of my throat. One slice, and it would all be over.

Like an alarm, the thought sounds again and again: *I HAVE TO GET OUT OF HERE.*

4

"Living room," Bowie says as the kitchen door bangs behind us.

I peek around, not expecting much.

My mistake.

Bowie has taste.

The canvas of drooping ceilings and crumbling brick walls probably wasn't much to work with, but he must have waved a magic wand. This place sings with beauty and elegance.

Two easy chairs upholstered in chocolate-brown leather flank a squashy velvet sofa. Oriental rugs in gold, blue, and red cover the floor, while black-and-white photos of famous architectural landmarks hang on the wall.

Bowie looks at me. The hoodie hangs low over his eyes, but the lamplight hits the bottom of his face to reveal full, sculpted lips. They're pinched at the corners like he cares about my opinion.

"It's gorgeous," I say before cringing.

But one of the things I'm learning about being in a dangerous situation is that the cocoon of fear is more porous than I imagined. I keep slipping in and out of it, which may be because part of me is excited to be doing something other cleaning and caring for everyone other than myself.

Plus, I'm also stuck here with that murderer, and I need to save myself so I can save Miriam. It's in my self-interest to feign politeness, pretend friendliness, lull Bowie into thinking I'm not going to escape, even though that's what I plan to do.

Bowie points toward the sofa. "Sit."

I sink into a cushion that's so soft it feels like a cloud spun from cashmere. We don't have sofas like this at home. For a while, we had bus seats and uncomfortable chairs in motels. Now we have a stiff floral loveseat encased in plastic.

He settles into a chair, tossing his legs apart. My insides skitter at just how big he is. I pull my legs together and wrap my arms around myself, enveloping myself in myself.

"I know you're scared of me, Snow White. You should be scared of me. But before you judge me, I want you to watch something." He grabs a remote from a table beside him.

The television jumps to life. On-screen, a silver-haired newscaster is talking.

"Earlier today, the body of Father Marlon O'Donnell was found in his parish church," the newscaster says with that grave expression people have when they're talking about something horrific. "He was stabbed to death by an unknown perpetrator. Photographs of young boys surrounded the corpse, and, on a pew, a dossier was found. It contained extensive documentation by dozens of men alleging sexual abuse by Father O'Donnell when they were boys."

On the television, a horde outside the church replaces the newscaster. They are waving their hands and crowding around the Chief of Police. He takes off his glasses, rubs his eyes, and then places them on again.

"Any leads?" asks a reporter so young and eager he's wearing metal braces.

"At first glance, the evidence suggests this may have been the job of a hitman," says the Chief of Police.

"In retaliation for the Father's alleged pedophilia?" screams another reporter.

"Probably, but I can't say definitively one way or the other." The Chief gathers his papers. "When we have more information, we'll release it. Until then, we're investigating every lead." He gazes into the camera. "If you have any tips, no matter how large or small, please call our hotline." The number for said hotline flashes below him.

I shift uncomfortably as I scan the room. No phone is in sight, which is a disappointment because I have a huge tip, and it happens to be sitting here with me.

Bowie clicks the television off.

I turn toward him. "Was he really a pedophile?"

He nods. "The worst. His victims number into the dozens."

"How do you know that?"

He sighs. "I can't answer that beyond saying I wouldn't have killed him if I weren't sure." He pauses. "How old do you think Father O'Donnell was?"

I shrug. "Eighty?"

"Close. He was eighty-one."

I nod, wondering where this was going.

Bowie leans in. Even though he isn't touching me, the heat from his body reaches me. I inch away from him in a desperate attempt to put some distance between us. I haven't spent time alone with a man alone outside of my dad, and I'm not sure how I'm supposed to behave. I've been taught that women should be modest and quiet, the keepers of men's morality, which they do by staying far away from males who aren't children or the elderly.

But how do I do that when I'm stuck here? I doubt he's going to respect my religious beliefs, seeing as killing someone is no big deal.

His tone goes harsh. "Do you know how old he was when he was first reported to his superiors?"

I shake my head.

"He was twenty-five. *Twenty-five*. Do you know what that superior did?"

Bowie doesn't wait for my answer. "Moved him to a new

parish. And kept moving him as he kept molesting more boys. His youngest known victim was seven. Father O'Donnell visited the boy in the hospital after he had his tonsils out and fondled him while his grandmother waited outside."

I press my hands against my stomach. "That's awful," I manage to get out. Awful doesn't sum it up, though. It's completely depraved.

"Nobody was going to do anything about it. He was too good at raising money, and that incentivized people to keep him around." He pauses. "I made sure he got it in this life." He slumps into the cushion, the hoodie dropping low over his face.

"Couldn't you have just reported him?"

Bowie gives me a sad smile. "Do you know how many times he's been reported?"

I shake my head.

"At least four times. Maybe more but not one less."

"Why didn't they do anything?"

"Who believes a kid against a high-ranking priest?" Bowie shakes his head at my expression, which is incredulous. "They don't. They never do."

"But why?"

"Because he was smart with his victims. He picked the ones from broken homes, with no one to talk to, who needed the hot meals and new clothes he gave them." He pauses. "If you're a police officer, who would you believe? A priest who's the pillar of the community or a snot-nosed kid? Even if the police officers did believe the kid, what were they going to do? Go after Father O'Donnell with a kid's word as their only evidence? The DA and anybody under him would have been toast."

"But you had evidence, right? If you have enough of it, they have to prosecute."

"Are you familiar with the statute of limitations, Snow White?"

I nod.

"As he got older and more powerful, he stopped." Bowie rubs his chin. "It's hard to say why. Maybe he felt remorse. Maybe he lost interest. Honestly, it doesn't matter. What matters is that the statute of limitations ran out on the victims except for two."

"What about them?" I ask. "Couldn't they testify?"

"One's in jail, and the other moved to Hong Kong years ago."

I don't say anything. Instead, I sit thinking about the boys, how they've carried around the shame and the pain for decades as Father O'Donnell kept racking up victims.

"I did it for the money," Bowie says. "But I also did it because it was right. And I'll do it again as soon as the opportunity presents itself."

I have to repeat the sentence to not just hear the words, but to understand how, like a math problem, what they add up to mean.

My body collapses as the truth smacks me in my gut.

Bowie is an assassin. He kills pedophiles. Because nobody will stop them.

Maybe it's because of what happened to me, what could happen to Miriam, but I don't think this twisted form of justice is wrong.

It's not right either.

Bowie fixes me with a hard stare. "Don't judge until I give you context."

"Context?" I whisper.

"I kill villains. You thought Father O'Donnell was bad, molesting dozens of boys, but he was a lightweight." He scowls. "Don't get me wrong. The world is only a better, brighter place without him in it." His volume increases. "I'm glad he's dead. I'm glad I killed him. And I'll kill more until the world is rid of them."

"How did you even find this out? To the point where you felt confident enough to kill him."

Bowie goes still. A couple of beats pass as my eyes dart over him nervously. Have I pushed him too far with this question? I've definitely touched a nerve, something that makes this personal rather than professional.

"I'm going to tell you something unbelievable," he says.

"Really?"

"Really. This group of billionaires formed a club. On the

outside, they do all the things billionaires do. They party on yachts. They date models. They buy ridiculous, expensive things like one-of-kind watches and three-hundred-year-old bottles of brandy." Bowie shifts closer to me as my breath catches. "But their real purpose is to rid the world of evil."

"By killing people?"

"Sometimes, that's the only way to make sure a bad person can't do bad anymore. They do and we do our due diligence beforehand. Nobody dies who shouldn't die." His tone hardens. "I save people by killing. If you'd seen what I've seen, then you would kill too."

I shiver at Bowie's words. He sounds so matter-of-fact about his criminality, like there's no big deal about a group of people hiring him to kill other people. I say the only thing that comes to mind: "Do you like being an assassin?"

His eyes narrow as if he's thinking of the right words to explain how he feels. "I make many people's lives better." He looks down. "But I take someone's life in the process, which is the only way to tip the scales from evil to good."

Without thinking about right or wrong, or how inappropriate it is, I reach to pat Bowie's hand.

He pulls his hand away before I can make contact. "I'm bad news."

5

B owie stands and strides to a bar cart where he selects a bottle of liquor and two tiny glasses. It seems like these glasses should crumble in his big hands, but he is so gentle with them.

He pours a quarter-inch of brown liquid into each glass before handing one to me. "Drink up, Snow White. We're going to need it."

At twenty-eight, I'm plenty old enough to drink, but I've never had more than the occasional glass of wine, much less hard liquor. So I hesitate when he hands me a glass. I need to keep a clear head if I'm going to escape.

But . . . I also want to seem cooperative to Bowie. Maybe he'll relax his guard and give me an opportunity to find an exit when his back is turned.

So I toss it in my mouth. The alcohol burns going down my throat and then floats through me, turning my veins into lace, my muscles to silk.

"Take off your hoodie."

I squeeze my eyes shut. I can't believe I said that. I guess it's true. Alcohol really does make you drop your inhibitions.

"Excuse me?" he says.

"Please take off your hoodie," I say in a smaller voice. "It's unnerving not seeing your face."

I expect nothing to happen since I have zero power in this situation.

I'm wrong. Bowie unzips his hoodie, and slowly, so slowly, he pulls his arms out of the sleeves. He throws it on a chair.

I immediately regret my words as my body temperature spikes. I assumed he'd have a T-shirt on underneath, something baggy and opaque. Instead, he's wearing a thin white tank top, the muscles underneath it visible and defined.

I swallow hard and tell myself to look at my feet. My eyes, though, disobey and drift upward to Bowie's face, which is . . .

I struggle to locate the right word because all the normal words like hot and handsome don't sum up him.

Bowie has dark hair and features that look drawn by an artist. His eyes, though, make my heart flop over—sky-blue and staring straight at me. He isn't just looking at me. He is *seeing* me, even the parts I never show anyone.

Get a hold of yourself, I say to myself, beyond embarrassed by my reaction. *You're mooning over a murderer.* I fix my gaze on a red swirl on one of the Oriental rugs.

"Can we talk now?" Bowie asks.

I nod. I don't trust myself with words. Who knows what the alcohol will make me say or do next.

"What's your name?" He continues to hold my gaze. "I can't keep calling you Snow White."

"Hannah. Spelled the same way going forward as backward."

"You've said that before."

"This makes a million and one times."

"What's your last name, Hannah, spelled the same way going forward as backward?"

"Einhorn."

"Okay, Hannah Einhorn, let's play a game to make this fun. You tell me three things about yourself. One of them is false. If I guess which one is a lie, then I get to ask you a question. If I guess wrong, then you get to ask me a question."

I frown. "What kinds of things are you talking about?"

"Simple, stupid stuff." He shrugs. "Your favorite movie. The name of your best friend. If you like chocolate ice cream more than vanilla."

"And the questions?"

His face goes blank. "That's where we talk about what we need to talk about."

I shiver, suddenly cold in the warmth of the room. "What do you mean?"

"You saw me murder a man. That's a big deal. One that could have repercussions beyond the two of us."

"Do you think I'll tell someone?"

"You might." Each word is hard and cold like an icicle. "Although it won't get you anything. In fact, it might get you hurt."

I gape at Bowie. "Aren't you worried about getting caught?"

He laughs joylessly. "Not even an iota."

"Why?"

Because, for real, Bowie killed Father O'Donnell in the wide open. With all the technology today, there's a better than good chance that a camera caught him going into or walking around the church.

Maybe it caught Bowie towing me out of the church. I freeze, hopeful for the first time that someone might discover I've been kidnapped. Maybe they even got the license plate number of his car and will be able to track me down using it.

Please, I whisper.

"For starters," Bowie says, "do you think the police want to find the guy who murdered a pedophile?" He shakes his head. "Justice was served."

"Don't the police have to try?"

"Oh, they'll try." He mimes scare quotes around try. "Which is to say they'll poke around the church for an hour or so in a half-hearted attempt to find evidence. When they don't find any, they'll file the case as unsolved. The news cycle will move on, and if anybody remembers, they'll be glad Father O'Donnell is dead because he's the guy who touched a bunch of innocent little boys, and the church let him."

"Don't you think a camera or two caught you? In the church, maybe outside of it?" I don't mention that I'm fervently praying that they caught me too.

"Starting twenty-four hours before the hit, they were rigged to show last week's feed. No one at the security company noticed." He half-smiles. "They never do."

They never do, I say to myself. Bowie must have a team of people he's working with.

"I might be a bad man by society's standards, but I killed a way worse one."

He's probably right. Why go after a bad man who killed a worse man? But even if Bowie did good, taking someone's life is an act of evil.

The worst. You don't need to be religious the way that my family is to know that's the truth.

For a second, I stop breathing. I have no idea what Bowie plans to do to me, with me.

The priest was a bad guy. I'm a good girl. But does that distinction matter when I saw a murder, am with that murderer?

"Ready to play?" Bowie asks, but before I can answer, his phone squawks insistently. He pulls it out of his pocket and checks the number. "Reckoning time," he says to himself.

I freeze, unsure of what "reckoning time" means.

"Stay put," he says. "I have to take this call."

Although I know I shouldn't, my eyes dart around the room, searching for an exit.

He shakes his head. "Only way in and out is the kitchen, which is where I'll be."

Deflated, I sink back into the cushions. How am I going to get out of here?

For a few minutes, I sit, stewing in my fear and worry. From the kitchen, I catch snippets of conversation from Bowie's end.

"No threat at present . . . Let me . . . Something odd . . ."

On and on, it goes. Obviously, they're talking about me, but I can't piece together enough words to figure out what the gist of it is. I listen for another minute, hoping for insight, but give up. Every time I get a couple of words, I lose the next dozen.

I press my lips together. Maybe I can use this unexpected time to do something that will help me escape. I sweep my eyes around the room, hoping they snag on a cord that would indicate some device I could use to reach the outside world.

Nothing.

I stand and, in a moment of inspiration, slip out of my shoes. I don't want my footsteps to give Bowie any reason to come back sooner than he will.

I decide to go through the room in a methodical way, but where to start? The console that the television rests on seems as good as any place, so I lower myself to the floor, inch by painstaking inch.

I squint into its dark depths, trying to make out what the bulky shapes within are. Using my index finger, I trace them. I know zip about technology, but I can guess that these aren't anything more exciting than receivers and cable boxes.

With a small groan, I cut my losses and move to the fireplace mantle, my fingers crossed that something might be lurking behind the collection of black-and-white photos that are lined up like soldiers. I lift a picture of the Brooklyn Bridge and peek behind it.

Nothing. Not even a speck of dirt.

I do notice one thing. The photograph is signed. I can only discern the first letter—J. The rest of the signature is a firm line. I check the rest of the pictures. They're all landmarks from around the world, shot in a raw, grainy style, signed with the same letter J.

Did Bowie take these? Is J the starting letter to his first or last names?

Maybe, maybe not, but at least, it's one small clue that could help me. I tiptoe over to his desk where a huge computer monitor dwarfs it. I shake the mouse, hoping that the screen will blink to life.

It stays dark. A quick scan reveals that the desktop is devoid of papers, pens, and any personal items.

That leaves one place—the desk drawers. A bead of sweat pops on my forehead. It's one thing to poke around someone's stuff that's visible in plain sight. It's another to go through someone's drawers, even if he is an assassin.

I listen to find out if the conversation is drawing to a close.

"I've got . . . Seven days . . . All I ask . . . can do."

Not yet, but he'll be hanging up soon by the sounds of it. And what that means for me is uncertain. The bead of sweat trails down my cheek.

I quash my ethical misgivings about going through someone's private space and open the first drawer. Nothing. The second and third drawers yield a big, fat zero as well, which leaves the bottom drawer.

I slide it open, expecting nothing. Instead, I gasp. A photo lays inside. It's one of those four-picture strips. Front and center is a girl of about thirteen or fourteen, wearing a black dog collar and such heavy goth makeup that I can't detect her features. Behind her is a young-looking Bowie of about sixteen or seventeen. The parade of pictures tells a story although I'm not quite sure what their relationship is. He's happy in all of the pictures, and her expression transforms from a grimace to a groan to a begrudging smile to a full-blown grin.

Is she his sister? A former girlfriend? It seems weird that one picture taken at least a decade ago is hiding out in a desk drawer. I start to turn it over to see if there's any identifying information like the name of a mall or an address, but I hear Bowie saying goodbye to the person he was talking to.

I slip the picture back in the drawer and dash back to the sofa just as he walks through the door.

"Sorry that took so long." He settles himself in the chair. He gives me a quizzical glance. "Everything okay?"

"I . . . um." I trail off. To him, I must look like a mess—sweating and out-of-breath. Plus, I forgot to put my shoes back on.

But I can't tell him what I was doing, so I go with the second-best truth.

"I'm scared," I say as I discreetly slide my feet back into my shoes. "I heard some of the conversation."

"It's going to be fine. I promise. You'll be back with your family in a week, maybe sooner, if I can get myself into a new identity quicker than expected. But to do that, I need to know more about you, so there aren't problems later." Without smiling, he meets my eyes. "Ready to play?"

This time, no squawking phone will save me.

6

I nod as I bite my lip. Nervously, I zip through my brain, trying to locate interesting facts about myself that might trip him up because I want to ask him questions, like *who else have you killed?*

The problem is my life has been so small that I haven't had many opportunities to develop myself beyond being a good daughter who cooks, cleans, and helps take care of my sisters.

Finally, I square my shoulders and cross my fingers. "Here you go. I have two sisters named Miriam and Salome. I hate the color red. I'm from San Francisco originally."

He gazes at me, his eyes going deep into my soul, prying out the parts of me I've tried to bury.

To cover my confusion, I say, "I've stumped you."

"Not even a little. Red is your favorite color."

My breath hitches before I regain my composure. He's right. I consider lying, so I can avoid whatever question he wants to ask me.

I don't. Mostly because I'm a terrible liar, but also because I want to play fair. I have a feeling that honesty is important to Bowie, and I want him to trust me, so later, I can use that trust to help myself.

"How did you guess?" I ask.

"I bet that red looks pretty good with your coloring."

His tone is benign, but I tug my skirt over my knees. I love red, but I never wear it since it's considered bright and attention-getting.

"It's time for me to ask you a question." Bowie's tone hardens. "You have to tell me the truth."

"Okay." I push a lock of hair off my face and look up at Bowie through my lashes.

He is staring at me, his jaw slack. He gives himself a little shake as his face flattens into a serious expression.

"Why were you in that church?"

"To ask Father O'Donnell a question."

"It was late. The church was closed. Why were you still there?"

I look down. A piece of lint is sticking up from my skirt. I roll it between my fingers as I decide how much I have to tell Bowie. "I fell asleep waiting for him to show up, and no one saw me when they locked the door."

He raises his eyebrows. "You fell asleep?"

"Under a pew." I press the lint down into my skirt. "I haven't been sleeping all that well recently, and it was quiet, and I was tired from sitting still for so long." The lint continues to stick up, so discreetly, I flick it to the floor. "So I took a nap."

"Was anyone around when you took this nap?"

I frown, trying to conjure up a clear picture of the church before I'd slipped under the pew. "I don't think so. An elderly man had just left, which is what spurred me to go under the pew. I didn't want anyone to think I was homeless."

"What did you need to ask the priest?"

"I thought you only got to ask one question." I go for a breezy tone, but the result is more like desperation.

I don't want to tell Bowie what that question was—still is.

"Help me help you, Hannah. What was the question?"

I take a deep breath as I frantically think of ways to edit the truth. "My family is religious. We follow rules that cover everything from what kind of food we can eat to how we should dress. And, for a while, I've suspected that we're being lied to and taken advantage of by . . ." I touch my lips as I try to figure out how to characterize Dr. Elías, the person who's directly and indirectly responsible for the mess I'm currently in. "A family friend who thinks he's a prophet."

"What religion is this?"

I sigh. "That's the complicated part. It's why I needed to talk to Father O'Donnell."

I don't say anything else, hoping what I'd said would be enough to answer Bowie's question.

He slants his body toward me as my stomach wiggles. I turn my head, so I don't have to look at him, notice again how good looking he is.

"Tell me, Snow White."

"It's a long story. A boring one too." I cross my fingers that he'll decide he's not interested and let me off the hook.

"I've got all night," he says. "You do too. So tell me about this complicated religion."

In my head, I do a quick scan to decide what I can tell Bowie and what I can't. I'll tell him everything except my part in it and what may be Miriam's part if I can't stop it.

In a low voice, I give words to a past I've never explained to anyone before. "When I was eleven, my parents went through a rough patch. The tech company my dad was working for closed down suddenly, and then the economy took a nosedive. My dad tried and tried, but he couldn't find another job. It was like he was being blackballed. Old coworkers ignored his emails, and all the recruiters who used to hound him day and night stopped calling. He couldn't even get an interview although he had a great résumé with lots of experience."

I lace my hands together. "Then my mom got sick, but nobody could figure out what was wrong with her."

"Did they figure it out eventually?"

I nod. "After a long eventually they did. She has Graves' disease."

He raises his eyebrows.

"It's an autoimmune disease that causes the thyroid to be overactive. My mom lost weight. She couldn't sleep and felt weak all the time. She fell asleep at work twice because she was so tired. They let her go after that."

I stop. I hate remembering this time when everything was so bleak and hopeless that it seemed like the sun would never shine on us again.

Bowie pats my knee, and the warmth of his gesture causes tears to prick in my eyes. I should tell him, *Don't touch me*.

I don't.

Because I need him to think I'm docile, I tell myself. I can put up with a little knee patting if it gets me out of here in the end.

I'm lying to myself, but that seems better than admitting the truth, which is that the pat felt better than nice.

He exhales. "How's your mom now?"

"Okay," I say. "But it took a long time and even more money to get her there. By the time she was stable, we were living in a homeless shelter."

"You lost your home?" Bowie's brows knit together in concern.

I nod. "A fire. To this day, nobody has any idea how it started since we were asleep. We escaped with the clothes on our back and my favorite stuffed animal."

I will myself still, so I won't have to remember the acrid smell of smoke, the shrill beep from the fire detector, the experience of watching my childhood home be incinerated by orange flames that licked at the black night.

"The stuffed animal was a duck named Quackers," I mumble. "We still have him. Anyway," I say, careful to speak in a neutral tone, "my parents thought they had up-to-date homeowner's insurance, but when they went to file the claim, the company had no record of their last couple of payments."

I corkscrew a lock of hair around my finger. "We were in San Francisco, and the housing market is bad enough when you're rich. Getting a new place is impossible when you're unemployed and have a mountain of medical debt. So we ended up at a homeless shelter."

Bowie pulls out a handkerchief from his pocket. He pushes it across the table. The gesture is so sweet, so old-fashioned in its gentlemanliness, that I almost lose it.

I'll cry later, I tell myself. *When I'm back at home, away from all of this.* I stare at the handkerchief. *Away from him.*

"That's a lot of tragedy in a short time," he says, his tone soft and consoling.

I quickly dab at my eyes with the handkerchief before shoving it back to him.

"It was hard for my parents. They had college degrees, savings, a nice house. Then, poof, just like that, it was gone." I hesitate. "My dad was suicidal. If it had gone on for much longer, he would have killed himself. As for my mom, she blamed herself. If she hadn't gotten sick, then we would have been okay because she could still work."

"How were you during all of this?"

"Not great. I had to switch schools, which meant I lost all my friends." I stare off into the distance, remembering the girl I used to be, who was lively and a bit of a troublemaker, drawing pictures of spiders on toilet paper to scare people and talking back to my teachers.

I twist the handkerchief. "I don't know what would have happened if we hadn't met Dr. Elías."

"Who is this Dr. Elías?"

"He's the reason I was in that church."

Bowie nods, encouraging me to say more.

"Dr. Elías had come to the homeless shelter that day to give help where he could. Within ten minutes of meeting him, my mom smiled for the first time in ages. Within an hour, we had our first hot meal. Within a day, he got my dad a job working at his charity. Within a week, we were out of the shelter and into an apartment. Within a year, my mom was in better health. Within two years, we had my sister Miriam." I finish up, "He gave my family purpose."

"What purpose would that be?"

"Dr. Elías believes the Messiah is coming. As in very soon."

"Like the second coming?"

"More like the first coming."

Bowie wrinkles his brow.

"For the Jewish people," I say. "Dr. Elías had a prophecy that he should architect the coming of the Jewish Messiah to prevent another Holocaust."

Saying it out loud makes me appreciate how crazy Dr. Elías is. How crazy his plan is. That after centuries of bloodshed and unrest, some random guy is going to be able to solve the problem using my family.

Bowie's jaw drops. "Why does he think that?"

"He grew up in a small town in New Mexico on the border of Colorado. His family had been there forever—as had a lot of other families, making their way to the new world after the Spanish Inquisition. These families had a lot of traditions outsiders would consider weird, like covering the mirrors when someone died, lighting candles on Fridays, and circumcising their baby boys. Everyone married each other—not brothers and sisters, more like cousins and cousins—which was considered important to preserve the traditions. This meant everyone kept exchanging similar DNA. Anyway, even with all the strange traditions, he was very Catholic when he went to college."

"What happened there?"

"He took a genetic test." I shrug. "He found out he was Jewish."

"And that was a big deal?"

"The biggest because Dr. Elías was majoring in history at the time. He was in the middle of writing a paper on the Holocaust. So he started researching the history of the Jewish people and tracing his lineage."

I raise my hands to deflect the criticism I know is coming. "He found out he's descended from King David."

"As in the David who fought Goliath?"

"The one and the same."

"How does he know this?" Bowie asks.

"Jewish people take all those begats in the Torah seriously. Plenty of them can research their genealogy back pretty far. There's even a museum in Tel Aviv that can tell you if you're a descendant of Dav—"

"Are you Jewish?" Bowie interrupts.

Reluctantly, I nod, nervous about admitting it out loud.

7

"I don't care, Hannah. Whether you're Jewish or Christian or worship some god I've never heard of. Whether you're white, black, green, or purple. Whether you're a man or a woman or identify as something else altogether." His sky-blue eyes cloud over. "When you've seen what I've seen, you learn that good and evil exist in every race, religion, and gender."

I exhale, relieved by Bowie's speech—at least for the moment. "My parents are Jewish although neither of them kept kosher or followed any of the other laws until they met Dr. Elías." I curl my lips upward into a pretend smile. "It took someone baptized as a Catholic to get them to practice strict adherence to the sabbath."

"What's Dr. Elías now?"

"He's Jewish, and he is observant as is my family."

"What made him decide to give up Catholicism?"

"History." I shrug. "It showed him that that the anti-Semites wouldn't care if he was a church-going Catholic. His ethnicity would trump everything. So he chose to identify as Jewish."

I take a deep breath to say what I know and my parents know, but have never actually given words to. "It's been hard for him. He misses Catholicism, the mysticism and the pageantry of it. It was his truth for so long, and the new truth, which is technically the old truth, doesn't fit him quite right."

I hesitate and then spit it out. "Sometimes, I think he wants to bring the Messiah, so he can get some of his Catholic beliefs back." I clam up because I know exactly which belief he wants to have back.

"Okay," he says slowly. "What does any of this have to do you being in the church?"

"Dr. Elías did his doctoral dissertation on anti-Semitism. His argument was that anti-Semitism is inevitable. That, although the Jewish people are occasionally left in peace, hatred follows them everywhere. Now, with all the DNA testing, he thinks anti-Semitism is going to get worse. He believes another Holocaust will happen, but it will be much, much worse because you can't escape your DNA."

"He's probably not wrong about that," Bowie says. "There's a lot of hatred in the world right now."

"That's how Dr. Elías felt—still feels—and he wanted to do something about it. He's worried the Jewish people will be exterminated before the Mashiach ben David came. So he's forcing the issue."

"Who's the Mashiach ben David?"

"That's the title of the Jewish Messiah."

"So how's he going to force the issue?"

I avoid Bowie's eyes. "Um, I don't know about that part. Just that he has a plan."

A plan that involved me and will soon involve Miriam, but I'm not telling Bowie that.

"The . . . what did you say the Messiah is called?"

"Mashiach ben David."

"So he comes, and then what?"

"The Messianic era will arrive," I say, "and the world will be in perfect harmony."

"Why don't the Jewish people believe that Jesus Christ is the Messiah?"

"It's a complicated answer, but the short version is that Jesus didn't fulfill all the Messianic prophecies."

"And those would be . . ."

"He didn't build the third temple because the second one was still standing. He didn't gather the Jewish people back to Israel, and he didn't usher in an era of world peace and prosperity. Also, believing in the Trinity is heretical to Judaism." I recite the list as if I'm an elementary school student giving a book report.

Bowie doesn't say anything for a while.

I get nervous as the silence stretches on, so I jump in. "Anyway, those *minor* disagreements in theology have caused a bunch of problems that have left a lot of people dead." I wince once the words have left my mouth. I sound glib and ignorant about almost two thousand years of blood-filled history although I was just trying to keep things easy between us.

Bowie rubs his head. "So why were you at a church if this is about Judaism?"

I can't tell him the real reason, so I tell him the other question that's been on my mind for a while. "To find out if the first coming for the Jewish people is the second one for Christians. And, if it is, then what does that mean for everyone?"

"You're sure you don't know the plan?"

I shake my head as I stare at a black-and-white photo of the Empire State Building resting on the mantle. "Only Dr. Elías knows."

He looks at me until I meet his eyes. "Your parents believe him?"

"With all their heart."

My heart drops into my stomach. I feel like I'm betraying my parents. They are good people. Gullible people. All they want is to take care of my sisters and me. But Dr. Elías is crazy, and they can't see it.

Won't see it, I admit.

Even if Father O'Donnell hadn't been a pedophile who had a deadly date with Bowie, even if Father O'Donnell had answered my question, even if I could have gotten my parents to see that what Dr. Elías did to me was wrong, that what he wants to do to Miriam is wrong, would they have listened to me?

No.

And it isn't because they don't love me, don't love Miriam, don't love G-d.

It's because, then, they would have to admit everything they believe is a lie built on more lies and that they've been had by a slick-talking, trick-wielding conman.

Nobody wants to admit that, much less formerly successful, college-educated grownups. Everyone thinks they're so smart that they'd never fall for the lie.

Until you're so down and out that the lie is the only thing that will lift you up and away.

"Hey, Snow White. Did I lose you?"

I shake myself from my increasingly grim feelings. I smile apologetically. "Where was I?"

"Dr. Elías. Why your parents believe him."

"Right," I say, trying to gather my thoughts and organize them into something coherent. "I never liked him. I still don't. But my parents did and they still do because he can out-argue anyone."

Bowie leans toward me. "How did you end up here? New York is a long way from San Francisco."

I stop. I'm telling him a lot, more than I should. But it feels like the floodgates have opened, and shutting them now would be almost impossible. Anyway, my story is so insane that Bowie might just think I'm lying.

"Dr. Elías said we had to let people know that the Mashiach ben David is coming, that they would be returning to Israel sooner rather than later. So we hopscotched the country to spread the news," I say. "From Los Angeles to Boca Raton, from Houston to D.C., we went anywhere that had a Jewish population. We never stayed in one place for long."

"Why?"

"Because Dr. Elías also was asking for money—a lot of it."

"Money?" Bowie repeats. "What for?"

"He has a charity that's devoted to building the third temple and providing assistance to the Jewish people who can't afford to get themselves to Israel."

"And people donated?"

I nod. "Sometimes, they wrote checks just to get Dr. Elías out of their hair. He would talk and talk until he wore them down." I smile without humor. "Cities got tapped out quickly. You can only ask for money from a minority population for so long before you're circling around to ask for more money from the same people."

"Did Dr. Elías tell anyone about his real plan?"

I shake my head. "He knew better."

"Knew better?"

"Jewish history is filled with people claiming to be the Mashiach ben David before they're exposed as frauds. Creating one would be unbelievable, pretty much the raving of a madman."

"So . . ." Bowie says.

"So he always talked about it in the future tense. He said the world is in desperate need of Messianic intervention and the Jewish people had to be ready when it happened."

"Is the charity legitimate?"

"Sure, as far as I know."

"Is New York going be the last stop?"

I nod. "It has the largest population of Jewish people in the country."

My voice fades as my hair falls in front of my eyes, a curtain closing the world into darkness. I've never talked to anyone before about Dr. Elías.

Because I didn't have anyone to talk to, especially not a handsome man who listens to every word I say.

Bowie pushes himself to his feet before sitting down beside me. I avoid looking at him as my stomach jiggles.

"Thank you," he says, "for telling me the truth."

I peek up at him, not breathing.

"You're pretty and a good talker." He half-smiles. "You're the best thing to be in this apartment for a long time. Maybe ever." Then, his face goes deadly serious. "Do you want to go home?"

I don't say anything because I want to say no. Not because I don't love my family. I do, more than anything. I want to say no because I'm tired of having such a small life devoted to the crazy prophecy of one person. I want to meet people. I want to talk about anything other than the Mashiach ben David. I want to stop pretending I'm into it when I'm not. Most of all, I want to get Miriam away from Dr. Elías before he does to her what he did to me.

But I have to say *I want to go home*. At this point, I'm the only person who can and will stand between Miriam and Dr. Elías.

"Answer me, Hannah. Do you want to go home? Because if you don't, I can arrange for you to go somewhere else and be someone else."

"I want to go home," I whisper even though the words together add up to *no*.

"Why?"

"Because my mom needs me. My dad needs me. My sisters need me."

"Who needs you the most?" he asks, his voice wheedling.

"Miriam."

8

B owie is a gentleman. He is giving me his bedroom to sleep in.

"I'll take the sofa," he says.

I open my mouth to say no, but Bowie holds up a hand.

"You're my guest." He laughs. "An unexpected, unconventional one, but still a guest."

He points to a door. "Bathroom through there. Obviously, I wasn't expecting company, so I doubt I have everything you need, but you should be able to take a shower."

"Thank you," I say as I take in the bedroom with its sleek, dark furniture. At home, I share a room with Miriam and Salome. It's cramped and cluttered although I do my best to keep it neat.

He throws me a half-smile. "Sleep tight, Snow White," he calls over his shoulder.

"You too," I whisper.

I take a quick shower and use my finger to brush my teeth. I debate what I should wear to bed. I've been in my skirt and long-sleeved blazer for what feels like a lifetime. They smell like fear and worry and the thousand other emotions I've felt today.

I decide on nothing to let my clothes air out and slip into bed.

Bowie's bed.

I curl onto my side, pulling the soft sheet up to my chin. I should use this time to think, to figure out how to escape, but I'm so tired that I snuggle up and fall asleep, like a bird in a warm, safe nest. My last thoughts are of Bowie: him getting the pizza I wanted, him patting my knee, him making me laugh even as we talked about deadly serious things.

It feels like a minute, but it must have been hours. I push through the black pool of sleep to end gasping. I'm wide-awake, and my pulse is racing.

Maybe it's the sleep, but I now see the situation in a different light.

I have seen a murder. I am a murderer's hostage.

There is nothing right about this.

It is only wrong.

And if Bowie seems sympathetic to me, it's because I'm deluded. To be more specific, I've got a bad case of Stockholm syndrome.

I flush at why, exactly, I've got this bad case of Stockholm syndrome. Because I've never exchanged more than a handful of words with a guy my own age. Because I'm lonely and desperate for contact with the outside world. Because Bowie is beautiful and bought me pizza and listened to me talk, and that meant something because I am that silly and sheltered.

My brain issues a siren: *Get out. Get out.*

Bowie doesn't have a choice. He has to kill me. I know and he knows that, if he lets me go, the truth will come out. All his bravado about not getting caught was to put me at ease, so he can figure out how to kill me in a believable way when I least expect it.

The game we played last night wasn't for fun. It was so he could see if I could lie. How well I could lie—even under the influence of alcohol.

But I didn't lie. And he knows it.

I bolt into a sitting position. *I am going to die*, I think. Maybe not today and maybe not tomorrow, but before the week is up.

I curse myself for my naivety that drowned out what Bowie

was really doing. All he had to do was pull the strings, and I danced.

I am not dying, I say to myself, straightening my shoulders. *Not until Miriam is safe from Dr. Elías.*

That means it's time for me to GO.

I gaze around the room, hoping my eyes catch on something that can double as a weapon.

My chance of fighting Bowie off is so tiny that it might as well be nonexistent, but I have to try.

A jumble of dumbbells lays in a corner. I tiptoe over and grab one. I try to lift it, but the stupid thing refuses to budge. With a strangled grunt, I try again, this time with more force.

Nothing. It's too heavy. I try a couple more dumbbells as sweat dribbles down my back.

Still nothing. They're too heavy as well.

I push my hair out of my eyes as I grasp the last dumbbell. With superhuman effort, I heave it off the floor.

Yes, I scream internally.

My elation dies. The dumbbell weighs so much that I start to stagger. It threatens to plunge out of my sweaty grip and onto the floor with a huge thud that will almost certainly wake Bowie, who will put an immediate stop to my plan.

I propel myself to the bed and thrust the dumbbell onto it. Without a sound, it sinks into the mattress, out of sight.

I sigh with relief.

Quick as I can, I slip into my clothes. I creep to the bedroom door and open it. Then, I rev myself up and curl my fingers around the dumbbell. I inhale and lift it.

My muscles strain so much that I debate putting it back and finding another weapon.

I don't. Behind the window shades, the world is lightening from black to gray.

Now is the moment because, in the next, I might be dead.

My arms burning, I sneak out of the bedroom and into the

living room. Bowie is sprawled on the sofa, his chest rising and falling in an even rhythm.

For a moment, I forget that I'm supposed to be escaping and just stare at him. Then, I remember where I am and what I'm supposed to be doing.

Pull yourself together, Hannah, I tell myself.

I'm almost to the front door when I step on a creaky board. The sound is like an ax striking a tree. As cold sweat trails down my back, I stop, sure Bowie will wake up.

He doesn't. Instead, a faint snore exits his lips.

I exhale, my body wilting with relief. I tiptoe through the kitchen until I get to the front door, which is locked tight. I count the deadbolts. There are six.

That's a lot, even for New York.

Unlocking them will almost definitely wake Bowie, which is the last thing I want.

But I don't have any choice. I'm going to have to unlock them and run for my life. It's New York, after all, the city that never sleeps. Someone is bound to be up, walking their dog or going to the deli for a cup of coffee.

Relieved to ditch the dumbbell, I gently place it near the coat closet. I take a couple of deep breaths to steady my whirring nerves.

Six locks and then freedom, I tell myself. I run to the handful of steps to the living room to make sure Bowie is still asleep. He is, luckily for me.

"Goodbye," I mouth. "Thanks for the pizza."

It's go time.

I twist the knob of the first lock, wincing at its clank.

I don't have a chance to turn the second because Bowie is behind me, then on top of me.

"Going somewhere, Hannah spelled the same way going forward as backward?" he asks. One of his arms tightens around my midsection as the other covers my mouth.

9

I'm crying, one of those big, ugly, messy cries after my failed escape, sure it's all over now. I'll die, and Miriam will be left to my fate.

Bowie wraps his arms around me. With a hand, he presses my head to his chest as the tears pour out of me.

I never cry. I hate worrying my mom and dad, and I always try to put on a happy face when I'm around Salome and Miriam. So I keep everything inside, squashing doubt and fear and disappointment one on top of the other until my insides got so full they split at the seams.

That's why I'm now smearing snot on Bowie's shirt and drenching him with my tears. He doesn't do or say anything beyond hold me. Every once in a while, he rubs my back.

It is wrong for me to be here in a man's arms I barely know and am most certainly not married to, but does G-d care, considering the options? The answer is probably because G-d has issued a number of rules, but I can't stop crying, so I don't move away from Bowie.

Even through my hurricane, a small part of me appreciates that he doesn't tell me everything is going to be all right when we both know it's not.

Finally, I run out of tears. Spent, I slump against Bowie until my body meets his. Shocked, I arc mine away although his arms and my arms are still knitted tightly together.

"I'm sorry," I whisper.

"You have nothing to be sorry for." He pauses. "For the record, I wouldn't have respected you if you hadn't tried to escape."

In spite of my fragile state, I laugh.

"You were going to hit me with a dumbbell so heavy you can barely lift it?" he asks.

"I was planning on trying. Were you awake the whole time?"

"Wide-awake. I had a feeling you would make a break for it."

"Why did you let me get all the way to the door?"

"Because you looked so cute sneaking out with that enormous dumbbell."

I blush. I doubt cute is the right word. Pathetic would probably be better.

Since we're talking, I decide to find out if my hunch was right.

"Bowie," I say. "Did you play that game to see if I could lie?"

"Pretty, a good talker, and you're smart too." He shakes his head. "What're the chances?" He brushes a strand of hair back from my face. "Couldn't you have been a little old lady? Or an ugly dude? It would make things a lot easier."

"Are you going to kill me?"

I go right for broke because I have to know. My head is still glued to Bowie's chest. His heart thumps in a steady rhythm. Whatever answer he gives me, it will be the truth.

"I'm not going to hurt you, much less kill you. I gave you my word, and my word is my bond."

My word is my bond, I repeat to myself. That phrase again. It must mean something to Bowie.

"Are you going to send me home? For real?"

"I am."

"How are you going to do that if I can't lie?"

"I don't know yet, but I will."

"The truth will come out. Eventually."

"Maybe, maybe not."

Bowie guides me away from him. He puts his hands on my shoulder, staring at me for a long while. He doesn't say anything as I gaze back at him. I feel weak and floppy, like all my bones have turned into rubber.

"It's early, but what do you say to breakfast?" Bowie asks.

My stomach growls. Mortified, I try to cover it with a cough, but I'm too late. The rumble echoes through the living room.

Bowie laughs. "You can't lie, and neither can your stomach. But first . . ." He offers me another handkerchief, which I accept.

"Thank you." I rub my damp cheeks before handing it back to him.

"Keep it," he says.

I stuff it into my pocket and look up at him through my eyelashes.

He stiffens as his eyes catch fire. The few inches of blank space between us heat up, like a burner turned up high. In the space of a second, Bowie recomposes himself.

"May I make you breakfast?" His voice is husky.

"Okay," I say unsurely.

BOWIE IS A GOOD COOK. Although I haven't yet tasted the mushroom-and-spinach frittata he's making, his confidence and skill speak for themselves. He's even wearing an apron, his muscles dwarfing the two tiny squares of fabric to the point where it looks like he's wearing a napkin.

He reaches for a knife as I shiver. An image of Father O'Donnell pops into my head, the blood—all that blood—flooding the church.

Truth keeps colliding with reality.

The truth is that Bowie is an assassin who killed a man in cold blood.

The truth is that the world is better without Father O'Donnell.

The truth is that Father O'Donnell deserved it.

But still. It's a brutal, barbaric thing Bowie did.

This truth does not square with the man slicing mushrooms as he hums a doo-wop song.

Reality is this, me with Bowie, feeling safe.

And I do feel safe. Whatever happens, I believe he won't hurt me. He's had plenty of chances to do something—anything—to me, and what he has chosen to do is make me a frittata.

"Think fast," he says. He tosses a mushroom toward me.

I stretch out a hand, but it whizzes past me. It hits the wall with a smack before sliding to the floor.

Bowie is right there, damp towel in hand.

"Let me," I say.

"You're a guest."

I roll my eyes. "An unconventional, unexpected one who is perfectly capable of wiping down a wall and throwing a mushroom in the trash."

Bowie tips his head side to side as if he's deciding.

I decide for him.

"Think fast," I say and snatch the towel.

Swiftly, I swipe it over the wall, palm the mushroom, and duck under Bowie's outstretched arm.

I chuck the mushroom in the trashcan. I turn to face Bowie, whose face is slack, his eyes dazed. With my hands on my hips, I smirk. "How'd the guest do?"

"She keeps surprising me."

"You haven't seen anything yet."

My body heats up. This isn't how I normally act, which isn't the same thing as saying this isn't how I normally feel. Like everyone, I have plenty of impulses, but I don't let them out. I'm too worried about my mom's Graves' disease. I'm too busy with chores and taking care of Salome. Mostly, though, I'm too scared about doing anything to upset the delicate ecosystem of our family.

But I left all of that to save Miriam from my fate, which seems to have ripped my spirit from its shrink-wrap.

In a week or less, I have to shove my feelings back inside and zip them up to my chin. So I'm going to enjoy being me—the real, sassy me—until I go back home. And that means having fun with Bowie, which would be off-limits in my real life but is fine for my pretend life, which is now.

The real, sassy me winks at Bowie. "What song were you singing earlier?"

He hums the chorus as I extend my arm.

"Dance?" I ask.

"What?"

"Your hips are twitching under that apron."

Wow, I say to myself, at myself. I have no idea who this girl is, flirting so blatantly. I have never once talked like this to anyone, much less a handsome man.

Bowie actually blushes at my words, two hot red dots on his cheeks.

"You've caught me, Snow White. My heart beats to the rhythm of a rumba."

He places his hand in mine and pulls me close. Our bodies fuse as we shimmy our hips from side to side.

I look into those sky-blue eyes that seem to see everything. I'm euphoric, an emotion I haven't felt in so long that feeling it now reminds me how wonderful it feels. I smile, my limbs light and loose. As the song swells, I tilt my head up toward Bowie, and in a way that feels completely natural, he bends his toward mine. At the halfway point, our lips meet.

During what is supposed to be my first kiss, I flinch. My stupid brain interrupts to remind me that I'm in the smelly clothes I've been wearing for over a day. My face is a blotchy, shiny mess from my epic cry earlier. And I can feel it. I have a crusty hunk stuck in the corner of my left eye.

Plus, this a huge no-no. I should not be kissing any man, particularly a professional assassin.

Bowie steps back as his arms drop limply to his side. "I'm sorry, Hannah. I got carried away."

In my head, I scream, *No.*

But my head isn't much use here when my heart is fighting against it—and winning too. So I don't think. I do.

More to the point, I kiss Bowie.

But I don't know how to kiss. I've seen people do it, sure, but I've never been sure what happens after the initial press of lips.

So I do that part with full gusto, gasping when we connect.

I might not know what comes next, but it doesn't matter because he does. He glides his tongue into my mouth. Gently, lazily almost, he loops and strokes and curls his tongue around mine as I melt into him, allowing our bodies to get confused with the other—where he starts, where I end. It doesn't matter. If someone asked me what I wanted to do with the rest of my life, I'd say, *this, only this.*

Squeak.

We pull away from each other and gawk at the front door, which is opening wide.

10

A black woman steps into the kitchen, a set of keys dangling from her fingers.

"Angelina," Bowie says. "You're early."

"On time, darling. I'm always on time."

Angelina saunters to the table. She is tall, taller than me and almost as tall as Bowie. She shrugs herself out of a cream-colored cardigan and hoists her waist-length braids over her shoulder. With a scowl, she perches on a chair.

I gape at her. Angelina is beautiful, all high cheekbones and deep-set eyes. She also has a posh British accent.

In a futile attempt, I smooth the wrinkles from my skirt. "Hello," I say. My voice is pitched so high it might as well be a dog whistle.

Angelina's eyes sweep over me. "Is this whom I'm babysitting?"

I twist a strand of hair around my finger. The use of whom makes me feel inferior.

"Do you come with seven dwarves, darling? You look like a fairy tale princess come to life."

I have no idea what to say to this, to her, so I shrink back until I'm pressed against the white wallpaper of the kitchen.

So much for being the real, sassy me. That girl has no idea how to deal with someone as classy and cutting as Angelina.

"Angelina." Bowie's tone has a low, knowing edge. "Be nice."

"We know *that's* impossible. Perhaps you have another request?"

"Are you hungry?"

Angelina fake laughs. "Food is for peasants. Anyway . . ." She points at the gloppy mess of eggs, mushrooms, and spinach that are resting in a bowl on the counter. "It's not like you have anything fit to serve."

Bowie closes his eyes. In one motion, he dumps the failed frittata into the trash. "Hannah, can you give us a moment?"

"Sure." I scurry out of the kitchen.

I'm not sure why Bowie asked me to leave since Angelina doesn't bother to lower her voice.

"What are you doing?" she asks in her cold, clipped accent. "Making breakfast with a witness? Kissing a witness?"

"I've got it under control."

"You have nothing under control. You are, in fact, out of control. Have you notified the Pact?"

"Of course I did."

"Then, do tell, why is Snow White still here, looking at you with goo-goo eyes?"

I flush. Guess I haven't been doing too good of a job keeping my attraction to Bowie under wraps. The attraction I should not, absolutely must not, have.

"I asked them to give me a week." Bowie sounds tired, like he's already had this conversation. "I'm going to sort it out. I just need time."

"And they agreed that you shacking up with a witness is the best plan for everyone?"

"No one had any better ideas. Anything else would require more people to be implicated."

Her volume increases. "You are in deep trouble. And, by extension of your error, all of us are in deep trouble."

"Angelina," Bowie pleads.

Then, she lowers her voice, and the rest of their conversation takes place in hushed, angry whispers.

I can only catch the occasional word or two.

"Not Hannah's fault . . . due diligence . . . the Pact will . . . putting together a plan . . ."

I sink into the sofa and pull my knees up to my chin.

Who is Angelina? By the way she casually sauntered through the door, it appears she's been here before. Many times, probably.

Does she know if his real name starts with a J?

I jump at the sound of footsteps. Bowie is walking into the living room, his eyes bright. Angelina follows behind him, carrying a shopping bag, her mouth arranged in a sour line.

He smiles at me and then Angelina, who glares in return. "The three of us are going to have breakfast, and then I have to leave to take care of a few things. Angelina will keep you company until I get back."

I frown. I like nothing about this plan.

Angelina swings the shopping bag in my direction. "Go change, darling. Your clothes smell like they came out of a rubbish bin."

Blushing at her takedown, I peek into the bag: t-shirts, leggings, underwear, and a hoodie in bright red. I rub the sleeve of the hoodie in between my fingers. These are normal-people clothes that will show forearms and legs—the kind I'm not supposed to wear.

It's only till I get home, I reason. It's not like I can say to Bowie and Angelina, *get me more clothes,* when I'm a hostage. Besides, is this the mitzvah G-d is going to care about at this moment? It's more important that I get home safe and sound so that I can stop Dr. Elías.

I also want to wear the red hoodie.

Angelina gestures at the bag. "Bowie asked me to get you a few things. He said we're the same size, which we are not, but I imagine you'll be able to find something that fits."

Bowie crossed his arms. "Angelina."

She fake laughs. "Don't worry. I'm sure we'll be braiding each other's hair and giggling about boys in no time."

She turns on her heel and disappears into the kitchen, her braids swinging.

I stare at Bowie, not sure what to make of the show called Angelina.

"It takes her some time to warm up to new people." He pauses. "But she is truly one of the best people I know."

"Does she know your real name?" I ask.

He nods. "She is one of three people who do. At this point, she knows me better than anyone."

Is that because she's his girlfriend?

My heart seizes mid-thump.

I don't like that idea. Not at all.

11

Breakfast is one uncomfortable meal. Bowie made scrambled eggs, fruit salad, and a stack of toast with strawberry jam.

I want to be a good guest and eat the delicious food. Instead, I'm pushing a glob of scrambled eggs around my plate, dreading the day ahead with Angelina as I relive the kiss I'd shared with Bowie.

The one positive is my new clothes. I have on jeans and the red hoodie, which I've zipped to my chin out of habit's sake. Since I'm not parading around in public, I reason with myself that it's okay to wear the one shade many Jewish people avoid. Plus, Bowie was right. Red does look good with my coloring.

Twisting in my seat, I glance at him. He's stretched his lips in a determined smile.

He puts his fork down. "So ladies, there's plenty for you to entertain yourself with while I'm gone. Movies, books, even a couple of magazines. If you want to make cookies, I've got all the supplies you need." He grins at us. "You two are going to have a great time together."

Angelina rolls her eyes. "Good god, Bowie. You're taking an awkward situation and adding glasses, braces, and a kick-me sign to it."

Despite Angelina's rudeness, I laugh. The zingers are funny when they aren't directed at me.

"Besides," Angelina says. "Do I strike you as the cookie-baking type?" She tosses one of her braids over her shoulder and throws me a withering look. "Snow White, maybe, but I doubt even she is interested in fulfilling your patriarchal ideals of feminine behavior."

Although I didn't quite follow what Angelina said, I smile because I think she just threw me a backhanded compliment.

Bowie and Angelina stare at each other as if daring the other to say something. Angelina opens her mouth, but I've had enough of their bickering.

"I'll do the dishes," I say brightly as I gather the silverware.

Angelina shoves her plate at me. She has touched nothing on it save a piece of toast, which has a half-moon serrated into one side. "If Snow White would rather be Cinderella, then who am I to stop her?"

Bowie stands. "I'll be back before dinner." Although his tone is smooth, his forehead creases with worry. "Have a good day."

"You too," I whisper, taking a mental snapshot of him, so I can remember the way his arm muscles curve and contrast with his straight spine.

"You too," Angelina mimics my breathless delivery as I blush.

Bowie waves before he closes the door behind him.

Angelina waits for the door to be fully shut before turning to me. "Spill the magic beans, my fairy tale princess. For whom are you working?

My eyes dart around the apartment. With Bowie gone, there's nothing technically keeping me here.

She follows my gaze. "Bowie locked the door from the outside with a key only he has." She shrugs. "I'm afraid you're stuck here with me. So for whom are you working?"

My mouth goes dry. Does she think I'm a spy? "Nobody," I manage to get out. "It was a total accident that I was at the church when Bowie . . ." I swallow, "killed Father O'Donnell."

I cringe as I replay my words in my head. I sound like a complete idiot.

"Why that church? Why that moment?"

"I haven't been in New York all that long, and it was the only church I'd heard of."

Angelina cocks her head at me in disbelief.

"Because it's famous," I add. "They always show it in movies."

"Where are you from?"

"San Francisco originally, then everywhere, but if you're talking about now, an apartment on the Lower East Side."

The corners of her lips lift. "Now we're getting somewhere." She leans forward. "Do tell."

"My family is religious and . . ." I hesitate, trying to find the right word. "Itinerant," I finally land on. "We ended up on the Lower East Side since that's where the Jewish people lived when they came to New York. Our apartment is not big and it's not nice, but it's better than nothing."

"That sounds dreadful. Why not go to a place where your money will stretch further?"

"Dr. Elías . . . he's the leader of my family . . . believes he's been called here to fulfill a prophecy."

"What prophecy is that, darling? Jesus is coming?"

"Close," I say, deadly serious. Then, I tell her everything I told Bowie about why I was in that church at that moment.

"It's a classic case of being in the wrong place at the wrong time," I finish up.

"I know you didn't mean to, but you've bollocksed up a lot of people's lives, including your own."

She closes her eyes. "If anyone can solve the problem, Bowie can."

At the mention of Bowie's name, I flush.

"You like him." She fixes her enormous brown eyes on me as I squirm. "He is quite likable. I'll grant you that."

"Are you dating him?" My knees pull together at my boldness. I really shouldn't be asking about an assassin's relationship status.

Angelina smirks. "How disappointed will you be if I say yes?"

I open and close my mouth, no sound coming out, which is all the answer she needs.

She tosses her braids. "Once upon a time, Bowie and I were together. But a couple can't be broken in precisely the same way, doing precisely the same thing to fix that brokenness. Together, the two of us created a black hole that sucked everything lovely into it. A relationship should fill your holes, not make bigger ones."

I nod as I repeat her words in my head. What are Bowie's holes? Angelina's?

"What do you do?" I ask. "Are you an assassin like Bowie?"

Nothing about Angelina says assassin. But I didn't think a man wearing a hoodie would be an assassin until I saw it with my own eyes.

"I'm a hacker, darling. I spend my days on a computer, finagling my way into private chat rooms where the worst of the worst people confess the worst of the worst sins. I access emails and private stashes of pictures that I pass on to people who can do something about it."

Angelina looks off into the distance. "Hacker is such an ugly word. It makes me sound like I just whack my way in and take what I want." She pauses. "It is much more elegant in reality."

For the first time since she's been here, Angelina smiles. "I'm something between a thief and a magician. I steal, and then I reveal." She pretends to pull a rabbit out of a hat.

I giggle. I'm starting to warm up to Angelina.

"The men I find are snakes, doing disgusting, immoral things. Bowie slices them in half, so they can't prey on anyone else again." She laughs, but there's no humor in it.

"How bad are the men?" I hesitate. "And women?"

"There are women too, but much fewer. The majority are men." She ropes a braid around her finger. "It's a good thing I'm close to Bowie. I would hate men otherwise, but he reminds me that men are good, too." She lets the braid slip from her finger. "Right and wrong have little to do with justice."

With that, she turns away, leaving me to ponder her words. Then my stomach rumbles. I'm hungry. Again. Maybe it's because I don't have the physical reminder of Miriam in front of me to worry my appetite away, but I feel like I'm starving all the time here.

Angelina is sprawled on the sofa watching a talk show. After our chat, she has gotten marginally friendlier. I don't think that friendliness, though, extends to having lunch with me.

But to be nice, I say, "I'm going to fix something to eat. Would you like anything?"

She doesn't lift her eyes from the television. "Black coffee. Be a darling, though, and put it in a nice cup, not one of those wretched mugs Bowie thinks are funny."

I go into the kitchen and start poking around for supplies. I find a tin of coffee, a box of pasta noodles, and the "wretched mugs," which are the type of cups sold in tacky tourist shops. He seems to have one from each state. I select a nondescript white mug for Angelina and the one that has Florida spelled out in palm trees for myself.

Were these mugs from states where he murdered people? I can't stop myself from thinking it. My appetite flees even as I continue the motions of cooking.

As I'm stirring pesto into my penne, Angelina saunters into the kitchen.

"Just like Snow White," she says. "Except, in this case, you've got a wicked queen to feed instead of seven dwarves."

"You're not a wicked queen."

Angelina arches an eyebrow. "That's a first." She settles herself on the edge of a chair. "I'm clearly too tall to be a dwarf, so who am I?"

"The Huntsman," I say.

She barks a laugh. "You're not wrong." Angelina points at my bowl of pasta. "I'll take one."

My eyebrows shoot up.

"To be sociable, darling. Eating alone is such a bore. You've been through quite a lot in twenty-four hours. I thought I'd save you that misery, at least."

"Thank you," I say.

Angelina's courtesy doesn't extend to helping me set the table, so I do that alone, lining up silverware and placing bowls of pasta in front of us.

I settle opposite her, letting my hair hang in front of my face. I'm not sure I want to see her reaction. I want her to like my food, which would feel in a stupid way like she likes me.

Angelina stabs a noodle with her fork and nibbles the end. "Bowie makes it better," she pronounces. "But this will do." She takes another small bite.

In my head, I cheer. We eat in a silence that's not uncomfortable although I wouldn't call it comfortable either. Technically, I eat and Angelina picks until, after ten minutes or so, the quiet becomes unbearable for me.

Although I've been feeling lonely on the inside for years now, I'm used to the external noise of my family. Salome whining, Miriam soothing Salome, my dad flipping the pages of the Torah or Talmud, my mom shushing everyone so she could have a minute's worth of peace and quiet.

To liven up my meal with Angelina, I try to think of a conversation starter, but I can only think of silly things like the weather.

"How did you get into hacking?" I ask, just to ask something.

"Because it is a profession that cares neither about my color nor my gender," she says. "My skill, which is substantial, is all that matters."

"Is Angelina your real name? Or do you have a fake name like Bowie?"

"Angelina is not my real name. It is, however, the name I took myself, and I consider it to be far more suitable than the name I was given at birth."

"How many people know your real name?"

"Two." She shoots me a frosty look. "And I intend to keep it that way."

"Why do so few people know your name? Don't you have friends and your family who know you?"

"They think I died."

"That's terrible," I say. "For them and for you."

"Dying gave me what everyone truly wants—the opportunity to be reborn." She shrugs. "I didn't leave anything that wasn't worth leaving."

"Are you from England originally?"

Angelina rolls her eyes. "How did you guess?"

I wink. "I'm lucky that way."

She titters. "I will say, for a fairy tale princess, you aren't completely insufferable."

I decide to take advantage of her good humor to find out more about Bowie. I want to know who he is, this assassin who can cook and dance and make me weak in the knees just by looking at me.

"How did you meet Bowie?" I ask, crossing my fingers that she'll answer my question.

"A long time ago, in a land far, far away." She glances at her coffee cup, which is empty. "A refill if you please. We're going to be here for a while."

Angelina sips her coffee as she looks into the distance. "Growing up," she says, "I wanted to be a dancer. A ballerina, to be more specific. When you're young, becoming a ballerina seems just as possible as becoming an astronaut or a pirate."

She waves a hand in the air. "Obviously, I, like many little girls, didn't become a ballerina. I didn't even have a chance to study. I did, however, absorb the idea of a ballerina. She is weightless, graceful, an angel who has alighted on the earth to—"

"Why didn't you get a chance to study?" I say, interrupting.

"Money, darling."

"Oh . . . I'm sorry," I say. I know what it feels like when your parents can't afford to pay for the horseback-riding lessons your eleven-year-old self desperately wants.

Angelina waves a hand. "Don't be. My family is filthy rich. I wasn't allowed to take ballet because it was considered terribly gauche for a wealthy young woman to prance around a stage in her underwear. I only tell you that, so you understand precisely how the sordid things that happened to me soiled my sense of self."

I put on my best listening face.

"While studying ballet may be considered vulgar, shipping

one's children off to boarding school was considered to be quite the thing to do."

Angelina strokes one of her braids. "When I was still a girl, I and Hop-a-Long, my stuffed rabbit, were sent to one. I was more naive about how people perceived my black skin than the average eleven-year-old, which made me low-hanging fruit for the bullies. One girl—I'll call her Winifred—took a particular dislike to me."

She shrugs. "It started with typical bully behavior, calling me names and ripping up my homework. Then it escalated into pulling my hair and hiding a frog in my room. She even stole Hop-a-Long. Now that left me heartbroken. I had one friend in the world, and he was gone. She did return him eventually, but she'd cut off his ears and tail." Angelina doesn't say anything for a moment. "It's not much of a bunny without floppy ears and a cottontail."

"Weren't there teachers around?" I ask. My life hasn't been a bed of roses, but no one ever mutilated Quackers.

My heart clenches when I think of Quackers. I got him when I was a baby and gave him to Miriam when she was born. Now Salome sleeps with him. He's family at this point.

"They turned a blind eye to it. They thought it was good for us to get knocked around. Toughened us up and prepared us for the harsh realities of the world."

Angelina cradles her coffee cup in her hand. "Then Winifred went too far. She cornered me after tea one day and started touching me. I screamed and pleaded with her to stop, but she kept at it. She was much bigger than I, so she placed a knee on my chest and started digging her fingers inside of me."

Her face goes blank. "I know now someone must have done that to her. Probably so many times that she became confused, thought it meant she was important when it meant everything but that."

I can't think of anything to say.

"I'm hardly alone in my story. What are the statistics today, darling? One in three? One in four children?"

"Does Bowie know?"

"Of course. He knows everything about me."

"Did he . . ." I can't form the words *kill her.*

Angelina shakes her head. "That would have been completely unnecessary."

"Why?"

"A prefect walked in on the situation who reported Winifred. Both of us were sent home immediately. While I received chocolate ice cream and a new bunny, Winifred was sent to an institution that specialized in difficult children. She had a nervous breakdown due to the tactics they used on her. Now, she's in the expensive version of the loony bin, her mind completely shattered."

My jaw drops.

"You didn't think this was going to be a happy story, did you?"

I shake my head slowly.

"Anyway, once I recovered, the most terrible thing that could happen to a pretty girl happened."

I widen my eyes in confusion.

"I went through puberty."

"Of course," I say in understanding.

"The story becomes quite boring and repetitive at this point, so I'll hit the high notes. An earl's son raped me at a house party. As everyone was enjoying their evening brandy, he pressed the pistol his great grandfather had used to pummel the Jerries with against my forehead. The boyfriend whom I thought I was going to marry became violent when I stayed out too late with girlfriends. He struck me so hard he gave me a concussion. A drunk uncle rubbed me under the table during a Christmas dinner, right before they served the pudding. I pushed his hand away, but he kept at it until I dumped my glass of sherry on his head."

She laughs without humor. "That's the event that set me on the path here."

"How?" I ask. Because out of the terrible things that happened to Angelina, this one seems the least terrible.

"Uncle Freddy was very funny. He could do everything from pun in Latin to use Cockney rhyming slang. He was one of the only people in the world who could make Mother laugh. She was not pleased when I ruined Christmas by accusing Uncle Freddie of molesting me."

"She didn't believe you?" I sound surprised, not that I should be.

Angelina gives me a withering look. "Of course she believed me. Uncle Freddie had been fondling girls for ages. She thought I should have been a good girl and not made a fuss before the pudding was served. Let him have his fun and be grateful it wasn't worse. After all, other people were there—people much more important than I."

I gape at her.

"Uncle Freddy was an asset at a dinner table whereas I was a surly young woman who wanted to argue about feminism." She shrugs. "The choice was easy for mother."

"Which was what?"

"To ignore me until she could be sure I wouldn't ruin the Christmas pudding again. She gave me a little money and told me to go make my way in the world. I didn't know what to do, so I spent my days at a computer cafe. Gradually, I made friends who did things many people would consider immoral but that, somehow, in the end, seemed moral to me. They taught me how to find the perverted secrets of people who make a living from calling others perverted."

"What perverted secrets? Who calls others perverted?"

"The perversions have to do with sex or violence. As for those who make a living from calling others perverted? Well, that's easy enough to answer. Clergymen and politicians, regardless of their affiliation, are the worst. In general, men in power seem to think their position enables them to a certain amount of depravity." She laughs without humor. "Sometimes, I wonder if that's their motivation to acquire influence."

She huffs. "People truly have not evolved very much since the days of cavemen. The internet has only made it worse since people can access anything their dirty little minds come up with. And if they have enough money, they will buy it."

"Yuck," I say.

"Yuck is right. The internet thrives on yuck. It, however, keeps time and date stamps of that yuck." Angelina says. "Hacking introduced me to a world where I could gather proof. Before that, it was always their word against mine."

She shakes her braids. "The word of a woman isn't worth very much in this world. But proof is. So I find as much of it as I can, and then I let people like Bowie act on it."

"Is that how you met Bowie?" I twist my fingers in my lap. It's been twenty-four hours since I saw Bowie kill a man, but everything I think about right and wrong has been challenged.

"Something like that," she says.

In my head, I run through her story. It sounds like something out of a movie. How could all these terrible things happen to one person in such a short period of time?

I look at Angelina, who's running her fingers through her braids. She has a small smile playing around her lips.

My eyes widen in understanding. "Did any of that actually happen?" I ask. "Or did you just make it up?"

13

Angelina claps her hands together a few times as she lounges in her chair. For the first time since she's stepped into the apartment, she looks at ease.

"Bravo," she says. "I see why Bowie likes you. Your ability to sniff out the truth is quite impressive."

"Why did you make all of that up?" I ask. "To mess with me?"

Angelina's beautiful face sags. "None of it happened, but it's all true."

I open my mouth to say something but close it.

Because I get it. She lied about the details. There was no girl named Winifred, and there was no earl's son. Even the stuffed bunny named Hop-a-Long was probably made up.

But she's been hurt—badly—by people who knew better, and it went unpunished. Hacking has become her vengeance.

"Thank—" I start to say, but I don't finish because Bowie is striding through the door.

My heart stutters. He's wearing a light gray hoodie, and it's unzipped, showing off abs that are cut like piano keys beneath his white tank top.

His eyes find mine. Without exchanging a word, we have a quick check-in.

I'm fine, I tell him. *And I like Angelina. She might even like me too.*

He smiles, relieved.

"Hello, ladies." He drops a few bags on the counter. "I'd like to cook you dinner."

"I'm afraid I have another date." Angelina stands and pecks Bowie on the cheek as he passes her the door key.

"Thanks for staying with me today," I whisper as she slips her arms into her cream-colored sweater.

She arches an eyebrow. "The pleasure was all mine." She shifts her gaze to Bowie. "Tomorrow?"

"Please."

Angelina's braids stream behind her as she sashays out the door.

Bowie clicks the six locks in place before turning to me. "So it went okay?"

I nod. "Better than okay."

"She's one of the best people I've ever met." His eyes sweep over me. "You're not so bad yourself, Hannah."

A hot flush creeps over me as I remember the kiss from this morning, the one that just got started before Angelina interrupted us.

Will it happen again?

I hope so.

Bowie, though, has other ideas. As he digs through the grocery bags, he says in a neutral tone, "I want to apologize for this morning. I got carried away, kissing you." He stops moving, a bag of fingerling potatoes in his hands. "I've been alone for a long time, and I've forgotten how nice it is to have a woman around." He dumps the potatoes onto a cutting board. "Especially one as pretty and smart as you are."

"Okay," I say, which is not at all what I want to say.

Using a scary-big knife, he slices the potatoes with quick, even strokes. I shiver a little. I'm still struggling to reconcile the Bowie who kissed me with the Bowie who kills for a living.

He shows me a package of butter. "I got the kosher kind."

"Thanks," I say although, at this point, I've broken so many of the mitzvahs I doubt G-d cares about what type of butter I eat.

"Can I help?" I ask.

He shakes his head. "I prefer to cook alone." He juts his chin to the table. "But I'd enjoy the company. So please stay."

I settle into a chair, tucking my legs up and wrapping my arms around them.

Watching Bowie cook is fun. All the white cabinets and counters look like a canvas that he's painting on. With a handful of salt, a sprinkle of pepper, and a stick of butter, he is creating art that we get to eat. In no time at all, he's sliding a plate in front of me as he sits down opposite me.

I inhale the rich, fatty aroma of chicken and potatoes.

Yum.

It's funny that I'm eating better now, as a hostage, than I have in years where everything is always half-off or a manager's special, which reminds me . . .

"What's the status?" I ask.

"The status?"

"Of me being here. Of you figuring out how to get us both out of here."

Bowie parks his fork on his plate and leans forward. "Your family has reported you missing."

A lump grows in my throat. "They must be so worried."

"It's only for a week."

"Why does it take a week?" Suddenly, the only thing in the world I want is to be with my family having a normal kosher dinner where everything is safe and understandable.

"Paperwork."

"What kind of paperwork?"

"I need a new identity. One that is believable."

I wrinkle my forehead. "What makes an identity believable?"

"It's not as simple as getting a new passport and Social Security number. I need a family, friends, a past that makes sense. It takes a few days to arrange that and pay the people who can make that happen. Plus, a crew has to come in here and erase any trace of me."

He gestures toward my plate. "I'll be offended if you don't finish."

I put a piece of chicken in my mouth, enjoying how the crispy outside enhances the cushiony inside.

"How long have you been in New York?" I ask.

"A few years." He leans back in his chair. "I wasn't excited when I got assigned here, but it's grown on me."

"Who does everyone think you are?"

"A nice, normal guy who runs a software consulting business from his apartment. A guy who goes to the gym every day. A guy who plays pool on Fridays." He looks at me and then away. "A guy who is unlucky in love."

My stomach twitches.

"No one suspects you're an assassin?" I manage to get out. "Not even a little bit?"

"I hide in plain sight, Hannah. We all do." He chews a bite of chicken thoughtfully. "The only way not to go crazy by thinking everybody is bad is to be with other people. So day in and day out, I go out in the world and interact with the world."

He jerks a thumb toward the front door. "It's one of the reasons why I like living in Queens."

"Why's that?"

"It's the most ethnically diverse place in the world. I meet good people of all stripes here. It reminds me that no race or religion or gender has a monopoly on morality." He eats a spoonful of potatoes. "I also meet bad people." He pauses. "Occasionally, I have to take one of them out."

"How often do you kill?"

He stops his water glass halfway to the table. "It varies, but usually a couple of times a year. It takes time to identify the target, gather enough information to decide if it's viable, plan the attack, execute it, wait to see if there's any fallout."

"How do you pick the . . . targets?"

"The Pact does the picking." He shrugs. "Generally, it's a recipe of people who have done terrible things, gotten away with those terrible things, and will continue to get away with them. Also, the Pact makes sure the killings will be clean getaways without me or them getting implicated." He frowns. "Some of the worst people in the world go unpunished simply because they're so well protected."

"Does it normally go to plan?"

He nods. "You're the first issue I've had. But that could be because it was such a public killing." He runs his finger along the tip of his dinner knife. "The Pact wanted Father O'Donnell's death to be prominent, so they could give his victims the satisfaction that his pedophilia was out in the open and punished accordingly."

"How did you find the pictures of the boys?" I squirm in my chair. What happened to me was different from what happened to those boys, yet I still wouldn't want anyone to know. Particularly Bowie.

"Some were from various police databases of boys, now men, who came forward at various points. Others were from chat forums where people talked about the abuse they suffered. We don't out victims. Ever."

Once again, there's that twisted morality, and I don't know what to make of it.

"How are the assassinations carried . . ." I trail off. I can't believe I'm asking about murder protocol.

"Home invasions," he says. "They're simple and effective. A blade to the heart, a few pieces of jewelry missing, a couple of chairs overturned." He half-smiles." I'm in and out in a matter of minutes."

"What went wrong?" I ask. "With me, with this one?"

14

B owie exhales. "The surveillance team is usually spot on when we do hits."

"How come they didn't see me? I may have been under a pew, but I wasn't hiding."

"They were a guy short that night. They figured it didn't matter since the church closes its doors at seven p.m. sharp in preparation for morning services. That day, the church had been practically empty. So they shortened their sweep. They only checked to make sure the entrances and exits were locked and that no one was lingering in one of the confessionals." A vein pulses in his forehead. "I didn't know until I'd already killed Father O'Donnell and had taken you hostage what happened."

I play with the hem of my red hoodie. One less shirking worker and I wouldn't be here.

"I'm sorry, Hannah. I blame myself. I normally double-check their work, but we were running late, and the Pact wanted it done that night."

"Why?"

"Because they needed to move the sweep team to another job." He catches my questioning look. "They're more visible. They spent a lot of time casing out the church, so they needed to get moved that night because people were starting to notice them." Bowie smiles at me wryly. "Now you know why we're in this jam."

"Are there other assassins?"

He nods. "Although the Pact is so secretive that I could be playing pool with another one and never know."

Neither of us says anything, so I peek at him out of the corner of my eye. He's taken off his hoodie and tossed it over the chair beside him. My eyes linger on his bare forearms, which are roped with tendons and veins.

Pinpoints of electricity flicker in my abdomen.

Stop it, I tell myself. *He kills people for a living. Plus, in a week or so, you'll be back with your family, and Bowie will be nothing more than a memory you can't tell anyone about. Your only goal is to get yourself home—alive—so you can stop Dr. Elías from hurting Miriam the way he hurt you.*

I wish I could listen to myself, but I can't. Instead, my eyes drift to his hands, which are lying on the table. They are big but perfectly formed with nails that shine diamond bright.

Bowie asks, "Is this too much for you to hear?"

I shake my head.

"I'm impressed, Snow White. Most girls would have fainted or freaked out, listening to me talk about killing people." He shoots me an admiring smile. "But you're right there, trying to understand, trying not to judge."

"I'm interested," I say, blushing.

And I am interested. In every single, solitary thing that has to do with Bowie. And it goes way deeper than how good looking he is. It has to do with him, his heart, which is different from anyone else's I've met before.

"What about you, Hannah? What do you do for a living?"

"I don't have a job," I say, looking down. "I haven't done any of the stuff normal people do like go on dates or get a college degree or learn to drive. I haven't even graduated from high school."

"Why?" he asks. "You're plenty smart." His eyes sparkle at me, which causes my heart to wiggle. "I know that firsthand."

"After we met Dr. Elías, my parents started homeschooling me." I hesitate, choosing my words carefully. "Once Miriam came along, they got too busy for it. Anyway, Dr. Elías says the only education a girl needs past the sixth grade is how to be a good wife and mother since, in the Old Testament, girls got betrothed at twelve, married at thirteen, and were mothers around their fourteenth birthdays." I shrug. "Anything else would be too corrupting."

"That's crazy," Bowie says.

I wink at him. "I thought so too, so I started teaching myself."

He grins at me approvingly. "How'd you do that?"

"It wasn't that hard because we were traveling in the world. It would have been almost impossible if we lived in Kiryas Joel." I catch Bowie's confused look. "That's an orthodox community in upstate New York."

"Got it," he says.

"In the beginning, I used to steal reading material: books, newspapers, neighborhood circulars. Once, I was so desperate for reading material that I took the instructions from a package of batteries. At night, I would hide in bed and read. But I got caught so many times that I had to stop."

"Were you allowed to read anything?"

I nod. "Recipes. Prayer books. A newspaper for observant Jewish women." I groan. "But they were boring."

"How did you keep learning then?" he asks.

I sit up. I'm pretty proud of how I continued to learn. "I listened," I say triumphantly.

His eyebrows lift. "Listened?"

I smile, stupidly proud to share how I managed to keep learning without any official schooling. "Dr. Elías would take me along with him when he was ready to close a prospect."

"Close?" Bowie asks. "As in ask for money?"

I nod. "Dr. Elías is smart. He made friends first with members of the Jewish community. He attended tons of *britots*—those are the ritual circumcisions of baby boys. He would get himself invited to Shabbat or, sometimes, Passover Seders. He'd impress everyone with his Jewish faith even after being raised Catholic. Once he identified the guys who he thought would be open to his message, he asked for money. It worked, time and time again."

"Wouldn't it be . . ." His brow creases. "Improper for you to be with two men?"

"My dad was always there, plus we did it places like kosher restaurants and Jewish delis." I stop as I think back through it. "We were like actors putting on a play, but we sold tickets after the show rather than before. Dr. Elías was the ringleader, always selling, selling, selling his big idea with even bigger words."

"I guess he was pretty good at it."

"The best," I say. "After just a few times of talking to someone, Dr. Elías could figure out what route he needed to take to get the prospect to open his pocketbook, whether he needed to talk about a future of hope or a future of hatred."

"Why were you and your dad there for then?"

"My dad was the proof. When someone looked like they doubted Dr. Elías, my dad would swing in and tell them our story, how Dr. Elías, a former Catholic, had reignited our family's faith."

"And you?" Bowie asks.

"As long as it wasn't Shabbat, he brought me along to write the receipt."

Bowie looks blank.

"Observant Jews don't use pens or pencils from sundown on Friday to sundown on Saturday."

"Why not just write the receipt himself?"

"He was asking *men* for *money*. It was much easier for them to say yes when a smiling girl processed their payment."

Bowie opens his mouth to say something, but I hold up a hand.

"It's sexist, yes. But I also got to spend hours in public places, listening to people talk. I heard lovers argue, friends disagree over politics, and girls talk about last night's date."

"Why did you do that?"

"So I could learn about people. What they cared about. Who they cared about. Why they cared. I know that a clique of women needs an enemy. I know that when two men argue about politics, they're actually arguing about status."

"So you learned about the world by listening to it."

"Pretty much." I laugh, waiting for Bowie to join in, but he doesn't. Instead, he's crossed his arms and is examining me.

I jump up. "I'll clear the plates and do the dishes," I say, avoiding his eyes. "Since you did all the cooking."

Bowie shakes his head. "Don't bother."

I look up at him, my cheeks hot, my insides burning. He reaches his hand across the table to end under my chin. His fingers stroke me as I quiver.

"You can stop telling me things anytime you want, Hannah. But, for the record, I want to know," he says. "I want to know it all."

I nod although, in my head, I panic. He doesn't want to know. He really, really doesn't. Because then, I'll no longer be Snow White.

And it's not because I've been with a man before. It's something different—and much worse. I close my eyes, already knowing how he would react, how any guy would react, if he knew.

"Do you believe that Dr. Elías has a real plan?" he asks abruptly.

My eyes snap open. I'm on shaky ground here. Dr. Elías most definitely has a plan. How far he can take it is up for debate. If it's up to me, then his actions will stop with me.

"Um, he has something." I sigh. "My parents believe it, and they're the ones that matter."

I open my mouth to say more, but I can't because Bowie is kissing me again. I slide near him, refusing to let our lips part for even one moment, as he knits his arms around me. We kiss until I think I might pass out. Black dots crowd my eyes, and my heart has taken over my body until I'm throbbing, wobbling.

I pull away to catch my breath.

"You do something to me, Han—"

He can't finish because the front door pops open. I startle as Bowie shifts me off of him. He stands, his hand around his back, his fingers gripping his knife.

A man dressed in tan pants and a button-down shirt charges into the living room. He's dragging Angelina with him, her eyes wide and crazed with fright at the gun pressed to her forehead.

My blood is thrumming so loudly I can barely make out what the intruder says.

"If you give me her," he points at me, "then I'll give you Black Beauty."

15

"That doesn't sound like a good deal to me," Bowie says. "How about you hand over my friend, and I'll let you leave here alive." He brandishes his knife. In the dim light, the blade glints with silvery menace.

The man in tan laughs incredulously. "You brought a knife to a gunfight, eh? Must be my lucky day."

Bowie gives me a quick look to stay put, which I do. But if he needs me later?

I almost faint at the absurdity of it. I would fight to stay with the first man who has me taken hostage rather than go with the second who wants to take me hostage.

Bowie walks toward the man in tan, his knife lifted. "The way I see it," he says, "you're the one with the problem, bringing a gun to a knife fight."

He stops a foot or so in front of the man in tan. "Who do you work for?" he asks. "It can't be anyone smart." He jerks a thumb at Angelina, who is cowering. "If you were, you'd want her. She's the one who knows all the secrets."

The man in tan squints like he's doing a calculation. "Maybe I'll take both of them." He smiles as if anticipating a big payout. He points his gun at me. "You. Come over here."

That's all the motive Bowie needs. Before I can blink, he karate chops the man in tan's outstretched arm. Then, he places his knife against the gun, aiming it toward the refrigerator where no one is. In the blink of an eye, Bowie lifts and slams his knife against the gun's barrel. The gun clatters to the floor and slides to the edge of where I'm sitting.

I hesitate for a second before reaching down and picking it up gingerly. Its weight is scarily heavy in my sweating palm. I've never held a gun before, but I know enough to keep my hand away from the trigger and to point the barrel at the floor. Quickly but carefully, I slide it under my chair.

I'm not sure if that's Bowie wants me to do or not, but I do it anyway. At least the gun is away from the man in tan.

The man in tan makes the fatal error of looking to see where his gun went rather than paying attention to the one thing he still has—Angelina.

In that instance, Bowie wrenches Angelina away from the man in tan, whose mouth plunges open at how fast things have turned. Bowie wraps one of his massive arms around the man in tan and positions his knife against his neck. With one swipe, the blade would open up a huge gash in the man in tan's neck.

"Still happy you brought a gun to a knife fight?" Bowie asks.

The man in tan whimpers.

"You've got one opportunity to tell me who you're working for and why you're here." Bowie presses the knife into the man's throat.

"Nobody," he squeals. "I swear."

Bowie sighs and adjusts his grip. "We both know that's not true." He rocks the blade forward until the tip is pointing at the edge of the man in tan's throat. With gentle pressure, he pricks the skin. A drop of blood appears followed by another. The man in tan squawks.

"Let's try this one more time. Who are you working for?"

"Jāzeps."

The name seems to mean something to Bowie and Angelina. Their eyes meet across the room.

"Why does Jāzeps want Hannah Einhorn?"

"Because she saw the assassination of Father O'Donnell. He wants to talk to her and find out if she's working for someone."

My head spins. How many criminal organizations are there? And how are they all operating without any of us normal people knowing about them?

The man in tan tilts his head toward me. "Seeing as how pretty she is, I bet Jāzeps might be inclined to do more than question her."

My stomach sours.

Bowie shakes his head in disgust. "Tell him Hannah was in the wrong place at the wrong time. Tell him she's under the protection of the Pact. Unless he wants a war he can't win, he needs to leave her alone." He pushes the knife into the man in tan's throat. "Make sure he understands."

The man in tan nods frantically.

"Crawl back to Jāzeps," Bowie says. "But I am going to take a little something from you." He feels around the man's pockets and pulls out a smartphone. He tosses it to Angelina, who catches it easily.

Bowie drags the man in tan through the kitchen and throws him out the door. The six locks click into place. When he comes back into the living room, his eyebrows are drawn together.

"Five minutes, ladies, until we leave. Not one second more."

16

W e drive for what seems forever. Through Queens. Into Brooklyn. Around Staten Island. Bowie makes lots of unexpected turns and keeps to side streets.

"Shaking any tails we might have," he says as he swerves through a fast U-turn.

Finally, we end in Manhattan near the United Nations in front of a stone-and-glass apartment building.

"Act normal," Bowie orders as he pulls into the garage beside the building. "Like you've been out having fun and are tipsy."

I pull the corners of my lips upward as I follow Bowie into the lobby, which twinkles under an enormous light fixture that looks like a constellation of stars. I peek at Angelina's whose smile is about as real as mine feels.

Bowie strides to the doorman. "12C," he says, pulling out his identification and showing it. "The ladies are my special guests." He winks. "Very special guests."

"Welcome back, Mr. Cooper," the doorman says in an oily tone. He fishes out a key and passes it to Bowie. "Will you need anything else this evening?"

Bowie leers at us. "I've got everything I need."

"Indeed you do," the doorman says as he checks us out. I flinch as, beside me, Angelina quietly snorts.

Bowie places a hand on each of our backs and leads us to the bank of elevators. As soon as we get it, he lifts his index finger to his lips. *Shhh.* He keys a code into the elevator panel and then presses his thumb against a scanner. It blinks green. He hits twelve, but when the elevator doors swing open, he throws his arms out to prevent us from leaving. He pushes twenty-one, which opens to a roof deck.

"Not yet," he says. We do this a couple more times, riding the elevator to floors that we don't exit until Bowie finally gestures for us to exit at three. Angelina and I follow Bowie down the hall to 3E. Bowie turns the key, and we step inside in a small one-bedroom apartment.

Angelina doesn't say anything. Instead, she stalks into the bedroom and slams the door behind her. Bowie winces.

"She's never going to let me live this down," he says. "At least we're safe here."

"We are?" I ask. The hair is still standing up on my arms after the terrifying experience at Bowie's apartment.

He jabs his thumb toward the door. "This is the only apartment building Israeli diplomats will stay in when they're in town. Bad guys can threaten the doorman and wave guns around the lobby, but nobody can help them because all the keys are numbered incorrectly. Plus the elevator requires a code and a thumbprint to activate. Even the smoothest criminal would be hard-pressed to access all that information, particularly on short notice."

I rub my arms. "Why did that man in tan want me?"

"I don't know, but it can't be good."

"Why?" I ask. "Outside of the fact he's a criminal."

"That man is the puppet of a criminal. The guy behind the curtain, manipulating the strings, that's who wants you." His eyebrows drew together. "And once he wants you, he'll stop at nothing to get you."

"Jāzeps?" My tongue trips over the strange name.

"He's evil."

"How evil? More than all the people you've killed?"

Bowie nods.

"Then why haven't you or another assassin taken him out?"

"There are three ways to deal with evil, Snow White. One is to ignore it, which is what the vast majority of people do. The second is to fight it, which is what the Pact does. The last is to profit from it." He sighs. "Jāzeps profits—more than you can imagine—from other people's sins. He runs a huge underground empire surrounded by a moat of men. Just getting face-to-face with him would take all the resources the Pact has."

"What does Jāzeps have to do with Father O'Donnell?"

"Father O'Donnell was probably paying him off, and Jāzeps is steamed he's losing an income stream."

"I thought priests took vows of poverty."

"Poverty is relative, Snow White. Father O'Donnell might not own a lot, but that doesn't mean he didn't have access to plenty."

"Oh," I say, cringing at my naivety.

"Normally, the Pact doesn't go after people who are involved with Jāzeps. It gets messy fast." He shakes his head. "Something really went wrong with this job."

"Why does Jāzeps want me? I'm nobody."

"That's what I'm going to find out." He shrugs. "It could be what the man in the tan said: Jāzeps thinks you're working for someone else." Bowie pauses. "But I bet it's something else because they can find that out easily enough."

"What could it be?"

"Are you sure Dr. Elías is working solo?"

"It's always been Dr. Elías. His idea, his plan, his execution."

Bowie exhales in frustration. "I'll do some digging tomorrow. Until then, we should get some rest."

"Wait," I say. "Why didn't you kill the man? Why did you let him go?"

"I only kill who I'm told to kill. Anyway, I don't want to deny Jāzeps the pleasure of punishing his man for gross incompetence."

Bowie looks around the living room, which is furnished with a sofa and an easy chair. "You take the sofa. I'll be fine in the chair."

I snuggle into the sofa as Bowie lounges in the chair. As he reaches to turn off the light beside him, his white tank top lifts from his jeans, and I gasp. Bowie has an inch-long gash that's congealed with dark red blood.

"You hurt yourself," I say.

"It's not a big deal."

"It is to me." I dash to the bathroom where, luckily, I find bandages and alcohol wipes.

I kneel beside him. "I'll take care of it."

He opens his mouth to protest, but I hold up a hand. "I've cleaned up Salome's skinned knees and scrapes more times than I can count. I'm a pro at this point. Plus," I point at the wipe, "these things sting. If I do it, I'll do a better job than you will because I won't be in pain."

"That's nice of you, Hannah, but—"

I cut him off by lifting his shirt, wipe armed in my hand. Then, I freeze. Scars march across his abdomen, thin vertical lines that rise from his hipbones to his ribcage. They're all in varying stages of healing, from the newest, bloodiest gash to a pearlescent one at the opposite end.

My breath stops, and my bones liquefy. I sink to the floor. "Are those . . ."

"Self-inflicted?" Bowie nods curtly.

"They look like notches on a belt."

"That's about the sum of it. But they're not there to celebrate or to romanticize what I do." He looks off into the distance. "I cut myself after I kill. Blood for blood. It reminds me of what I'm doing. That I shouldn't take it lightly."

I dab at the gash and then press a bandage against, taking care to use light, almost nonexistent pressure.

"Thank you," he says.

I take my finger and trace the wound farthest away from the newest. As if playing a glissando on the piano, I sweep my hands across the scars, their shades darkening from white to red.

Bowie tenses, but I don't stop until I reach the newest one. Then, I dip my head and kiss the bandage. "A kiss to help you feel better," I say. I've kissed about a hundred of Salome's boo-boos, but this connection of my lips to Bowie's cut goes much deeper than that. I'm trying to make him feel better, not just on the outside, but the inside too.

I step outside myself for a moment. If anyone saw me, they would freak out—for a good reason. I've known Bowie for approximately two days, and I'm worried about making a guy who kills other guys feel better.

And yet everything I thought before I met Bowie is not what I think now.

"You have fifteen scars," I say. "How many will be enough?"

"Seventeen. That's when I quit."

"Why seventeen?"

"Because the pervert who caused my sister's death had seventeen victims."

Bowie yanks his shirt down. "That's way more than I should have told you."

"I want to know," I say. "I want to know everything."

He shakes his head. "You don't." He reaches out and strokes the underside of my chin. His touch is delicate, yet it feels like he's trailing a struck match over my skin.

"The more you know, the harder it's going to be to get you home." His flicker over me. "That's what you want, right? To go home."

I don't say anything.

"Do you want to go home, Hannah?" he repeats.

I square my shoulders and tell Bowie the truth. "I don't want to, but I have to. Miriam's life depends on it."

"Then I'll get you home."

Buoyed by my decisions, I take Bowie's hand. "I want to know. Everything."

"It's not a pretty story," he says.

17

I rest my head on Bowie's shoulder and wrap my arms around his massive bulk. I press myself against him until our connected bodies have squeezed out any air. All that's left is our hearts beating against each other.

I want to give Bowie my physical presence, to offer him comfort in preparation for whatever awful story he's about to tell me.

Bowie exhales. "I haven't told the story in so long that I'm not sure where to begin."

I think for a moment to see if I can help him find a point of entry. "What's your happiest childhood memory?"

"It's a stupid one, just an ordinary day in October. The sky was blue, the air was crisp, and the trees were the color of pumpkins. My dad took me out hunting—"

"Hunting?"

"I grew up in a rural area, so hunting's a big thing." He sees my confused look. "I know you're a city slicker, but plenty of people in America still hunt to eat." He half-smiles. "Regardless, it's not about going into the woods and shooting the first wild animal you see. There are ethics. My dad taught me to respect the game and to follow the laws that keep everyone safe."

I nod, encouraging him to say more.

"It's how I learned to use knives. It's an act of disrespect to hack an animal to bits after you've killed it. I always treated my game as works of art to be honored."

I don't know much about hunting, but what Bowie is talking about reminds me of *shechita*, which is the Jewish method of slaughter. The procedure causes a rapid drop in blood pressure in the brain, so the animal is unconscious and doesn't feel pain. It's designed to be respectful, humane, and lawful.

Bowie looks off into the distance as if picturing the perfect fall day in his mind. "That was the first time I shot a buck. My dad was so proud of me that he almost cried. When we came dragging it home on top of our pickup truck, I was so excited that I rode in the bed, so I could see it."

"Do you still hunt?" I ask before burying my face into Bowie's chest.

I'm an idiot. Of course, he still hunts. But his prey is perverts rather than animals.

Bowie strokes my hair. "Even assassins get vacations. When I get a chance, I fly to places that need help managing their deer populations."

"Can your dad go with you?"

The muscles in his chest bunch up. "He can't."

I rub my cheek against his chest. "I'm sorry."

"It's okay," he says in a tone that means anything but. "Anyway, I butchered the buck and made dinner for everyone. We sat around the table, eating and laughing until almost midnight."

"Everyone would be who?"

"My mom, dad, and younger sister." He laughs. "My mom's a terrible cook. She could burn water. As for my dad, he refused to follow a recipe. He would double some things and halve others. Every once in a while, he'd make something good, which would give him just enough confidence to keep cooking."

I make a mental note that Bowie is talking about his mom in the present tense and his dad in the past. I still don't know about his sister. That is, if Bowie is telling me the truth and not pulling an Angelina.

"What's your sister's name?" I ask, hoping for an answer that will go beyond the question.

"Emily."

It's not what I wanted, but it is a new piece of the puzzle named Bowie.

"Finally, when I was a teenager, I'd had enough," he says. "It's hard to believe now, but I once looked like a skeleton."

I trace my finger over the bowling ball curve of his bicep. "That is hard to believe."

"I went to the library and checked out every cookbook they had. I got good, mostly because I was hungry."

"Your family must have been grateful."

"They were. Dinner became the best part of the day."

I want to say, *The most beautiful things in life are the simplest.*

I don't because it sounds cheesy, like something from a greeting card. It doesn't matter because Bowie seems to be thinking the same thing. He drops a kiss on top of my head.

"I was so happy that I didn't notice someone wasn't," he says in a low voice.

"Who was that?"

"My sister. She was what we used to call high strung back then. She got the blues easily, would be down for days. Today, someone would recognize it for what it was."

"Which was?"

"Depression." He pauses. "Mom has spells too."

I tighten my arms around Bowie's chest.

"I'd always felt protective of Emily. She was sickly as a baby, and I remember holding her in my arms when I was all of three years old. She felt lighter than my favorite stuffed dinosaur, and I promised her, right then and there, I would always be around to protect her." He looks down. "At that age, I didn't understand what it meant to give someone your word as your bond." He pauses. "I do now."

I rub my face against Bowie, understanding exactly what it means to be young and not understand what you've committed yourself to.

"Emily was going through a hard time. Her best friend had moved away, and she was failing a couple of classes. A guy she went to a school dance with ignored her for weeks afterward. At thirteen, it felt like her world was ending. She started spending more and more time alone. To make sure no one bothered her, which is to say that no one got close enough to hurt her, she started dressing like a goth. Black clothing, heavy eye makeup, a collar with studs." He laughs sadly. "She looked like a puppy trying to be a Rottweiler, which is why my folks let her be. They figured she'd grow out of it."

I shudder as I remember being twelve. It'd been better than eleven, but mostly because my parents were happier, not because I was.

"Right around this time, a new neighbor moved next door. We lived in a small town, so a new neighbor was big news."

Bowie stops talking.

This must be where the story goes south.

18

I press myself against Bowie, letting him know that I'm not leaving no matter how bad his story gets.

He takes a deep breath and continues. "Mr. Wilson was a widower, and he seemed like the nicest guy in the world. He'd mow our lawn, just because. He'd drop off tomatoes from his garden. He'd pay me a few bucks to wash his car and then give me a big tip afterward. In no time at all, he became family. We had him over for dinner and gave him a key to check on things when we went out of town to visit my grandma."

Bowie's voice hardens. "We never asked for the key back. Because that's not what neighbors do." He slams a hand down on an armrest. "I think all the time about what would have happened if we'd asked for that key back."

I place my hand on top of his, which is shaking with rage and regret.

"One random day, in the middle of summer, he let himself into our house and raped Emily. She'd been feeling depressed, so she stayed in to watch TV and sleep."

Bowie has pitched his voice so low that I can barely hear him.

"He knew what he was doing. He used a condom. He threw her

in a bath afterward as she cried. As for his fingerprints, which were everywhere over our house? Well, that was easy to explain. He was our trusted neighbor with his own house key. In fact, he'd just been over for dinner the night before."

I stroke Bowie's back.

"To my parents' everlasting credit, they believed Emily. My dad stormed down to the police station and demanded they arrest Mr. Wilson. As you can imagine, that caused a problem for the officer on duty. Emily had been caught skipping school to smoke a cigarette in the woods while the cop went to church with Mr. Wilson. They were in a men's Bible study group together."

Bowie inhaled. "It was an open-and-shut case to him," he says. "But he did have an obligation to go through the motions. He questioned Emily, which is to say he argued with her version of events."

Inside, my heart collapses for Bowie's sister as I remember Angelina's words. *The word of a woman isn't worth very much in this world.*

"He poked enough holes in Emily's story, so he could feel good about calling it a misunderstanding," Bowie says. "It didn't help that Mom was there, yelling at him to stop asking questions and go arrest Mr. Wilson."

"What kind of holes?"

"She couldn't remember exactly what time it was, only that it was afternoon. She couldn't remember if she was wearing a T-shirt with a V-neck or a scooped one. She couldn't remember if Mr. Wilson let himself out the front door or the back door. She didn't know why she didn't call the police immediately if she really, truly had been raped and wasn't making up a story for the fun of ruining a man's life."

"That's a huge burden to put on a thirteen-year-old victim," I say. "Take mental notes while you're being raped, so you can retell it later in the hopes that, if you have enough details, they'll believe you."

"That's about right."

"What about DNA evidence? I mean, she lost her virginity. Wouldn't that have clued them in?"

He presses his lips together. "My parents had never heard of a rape kit. Even if they had, I'm not sure the hospital would have had one. They were equipped for births and heart attacks. We'd probably have to go to the one a few hours away, and Emily was not up for traveling at that point."

"What happened?" I ask in a small voice? "After all this?"

"She hung herself." Bowie's body tenses. "Word had gotten out that she'd seduced nice Mr. Wilson, and she couldn't bear to go back to school after that. The kids were so mean, writing graffiti on her locker and taunting her in the hall."

I gasp.

"She didn't leave a note, but we didn't need one. My dad lost his mind. There was no reasoning with him because his little girl was dead. He took his hunting rifle and shot Mr. Wilson to death."

I want to say something, anything, but I can't find the words that will alleviate the horror.

"When the police investigated the scene, they found a computer." Bowie's voice takes on an exhausted, resigned tone. "On it was a diary with dates, locations, names, even candid pictures of the girls. After reading it, they figured out he'd done this sixteen times. My sister was number seventeen. Every year or so, he'd move to a new town and tell the same sad story that he was a lonely widower who wanted to be around good, God-fearing people."

"How come he wasn't caught before this? Sixteen is a lot of girls. I can't believe nobody came forward."

"As they say in real estate, location, location, location."

I wrinkle my forehead. "Location, location, location?"

"He knew how to pick the right places, towns that were small and tight-knit, where everybody knew everybody else. He'd work his way into the community by joining the church and buying out the bake sale—always being the nicest guy you'd ever meet. As he was pulling the wool over everyone's eyes, he'd start looking for his victim. Once he found her, he'd start grooming the family. He'd get himself invited over to dinner, and he'd offer to housesit when they went on vacation. Girls from religious families were good victims because of the emphasis on purity. They would never tell because then everyone would know they weren't a virgin anymore."

My breath starts to come faster and faster. Technically, I'm a virgin although . . .

I force myself to inhale slowly. This isn't the time to think about myself. Not when Bowie is spilling his guts to me.

"Why did he pick Emily?" I ask. "She doesn't sound like his normal victim."

"Always so smart, Hannah. She wasn't. I think he was bored. He'd gotten away with it sixteen times, and he wanted something different. Plus, under the goth makeup, my sister was a very pretty girl."

"Yuck," I say.

"Pedophiles don't think like normal people. They only care about what they want and not getting caught so that they can do it again."

"What happened to your dad?"

"He went to jail. The judge was sorry about it, seeing as my dad had lost his daughter and exposed a serial pedophile, but he'd killed a man. The sentence was lenient, not that it mattered. Dad was like a balloon that'd been stuck with a pin. He had a heart attack less than a year later."

I'm crying. Not for me, oh no. For Bowie. For his sister. For his mom and dad. For the ways that one evil person could ruin so many lives.

"It's okay, Hannah."

"It's not okay. There's nothing about this story that is okay."

We cling to each other for a while, not saying anything.

"Where's your mom?" I ask.

"Still there. She won't leave the graves."

"Is that why you became a . . ." My lips refuse to form the word assassin.

"Nobody got justice in that situation. Not my sister. Not my dad. Not Mr. Wilson. So I took justice into my own hands."

"How did you do that?" I ask.

"By hanging out in chat rooms and joining groups that would make your hair stand on end," he says. "But I learned the hard-and-fast rule of the internet."

"Which is what?"

"Because it's anonymous, people talk big, but they don't always act big." He frowns. "I was so confident going in to my first kill. But when I showed up, the guy had nothing. He had done nothing. He had fantasies, sure, but he'd never acted on them. He got off listening to other people's actions."

"You didn't do anything?"

"I called in an anonymous tip." He shrugs. "I doubt it got investigated, but I wasn't going to take a man's life for talking stupid on an Internet forum."

"Is that how you met Angelina?"

He nods. "We needed each other. She could identify the perpetrator and assemble proof. I could do something about it. Two hits later, the Pact offered us jobs."

"Why do you kill with a knife?" I asked. "Wouldn't a gun be easier?"

"Probably. But it's the weapon I'm comfortable with."

I shiver. Bowie doesn't sound like Bowie anymore. A bead of cold sweat forms on my forehead and trickles down my cheek to end on Bowie's tank top.

He places his hands under my armpits and lifts me until we're facing each other. His eyes find mine.

"What do you think of me now, Snow White?" He tries for a casual tone, but the result is harsh, brutish. His eyes close.

He thinks I'm going to reject him. That he'll finally get the chance to validate the story he's told himself about himself. That he's a bad, broken man.

I'm not giving him that chance.

"I think you're wonderful," I say.

Bowie checks me out for signs of lying, but he already knows he's not going to find them.

19

B owie and I sleep together in a tangle of limbs.

Not sleep-sleep together. Angelina is in the bedroom a dozen feet away. Plus, I'm not ready for that yet. With my past, I'm not sure I will be ready for it before it's time for me to go back to my family. Then Bowie would know the truth about me, and I don't want that. I love being his Snow White.

Instead, Bowie has made us a makeshift bed on the floor since the sofa is too small for both of us. He lies down, and I fit my body into his, filling his spaces, having mine filled. I don't feel complete, but expanded, like with him, I can do more, be more.

I would have stayed like that forever if it isn't for Angeline swinging open the bedroom door and stomping into the living room.

I push myself through the black film of sleep to meet Angelina's eyes, which are livid.

I sit up, smoothing down my t-shirt and dragging a hand through the knots in my hair.

"Good morning," I whisper.

Angelina tosses her braids. "There's nothing good about this morning, darling."

She swings her gaze to Bowie. "We have work to do."

He stiffens beside me. Reluctantly, we peel our bodies apart and sit up.

Angelina's lips narrow as she studies our clothed bodies and serious expressions. She nods slightly, and a sunbeam pokes through the dark clouds of her eyes.

Because I didn't sleep-sleep with Bowie.

This has earned me a point with Angelina.

"I'll see if I can find some breakfast for us," I say and scurry to the kitchen.

The kitchen is tiny but opulent with high-end appliances, marble countertops, and cabinetry as sleek and dark as a mink coat.

The first cabinet is spring-loaded, and I jump back when it swings open. It is groaning with end-of-days supplies: cans of vegetable soup, boxes of ramen noodles, tins of coffee. The next one holds dried fruit in shrink-wrapped packages and containers of evaporated milk. I poke through the rest of the kitchen, finding batteries, flashlights, and enough bottled water to keep all of New York City hydrated for a week.

Since the only thing needed to make these supplies edible is boiling water, I find a kettle, fill it to the brim, and put it on the stove. At least it's not the actual end of days where I'd have to rub two sticks together to make a fire.

When I deliver breakfast to Bowie and Angelina, they're at the dining room table, huddled around a computer, the man in tan's phone plugged into it.

"Breakfast," I say in a cheery voice, plopping down bowls of oatmeal and mugs of coffee next to them.

They ignore me, their eyes fixed on the computer screen. Finally, Bowie lifts his eyes and nods a quick thank you.

My spine bows. I am useless. With my head down, I look up at Angelina and Bowie, who are competent and in control. I'm worse than useless because I'm the one who got everyone into this mess.

I trudge back into the kitchen and eat my tasteless oatmeal and drink my bitter tea standing up.

I want to help myself, help Bowie and Angelina, but there's nothing to do beyond pour coffee and make meals as they try to put together why the man in tan showed up to take me to Jāzeps.

They pore over the computer, take calls in the bedroom, and furiously whisper as I pace the same circle from the kitchen to the living room. Sometimes, I sit and stare at the East River where boats lazily loop Manhattan, gaggles of tourists hanging from their decks and snapping photos. Once, I take a nap in the bedroom, welcoming the hour of blankness where I'm not feeling guilty for my part in the whole thing.

Finally, Bowie and Angelina raise their heads. Their eyes are bleary, their expressions wilted.

"You're in trouble, darling," Angelina says. "More than you can possibly fathom."

WE GATHER around the dining room table like it's a funeral as our bowls of ramen get colder and colder.

"What's going on?" I twist my hands in my lap. "Why am I in trouble? What kind of trouble am I in? How do I . . ." I swallow. "Get myself out of trouble?"

Angelina spears one noodle on her fork and, daintily, slurps it down. She pushes the bowl away. "Jāzeps knows who you are," she says. "As far as we can tell, he's known about you for years." Angeline pulls her braids over a shoulder. "He has, in fact, been following you for years."

"Me?" I squeak.

"Perhaps not you exclusively. But your family."

Angelina fixes her dark gaze on me. "Why don't you tell us what you know?"

"I don't know anything." I look down at my hands, my fingers wrapped around each other. "I really don't."

That's not true. I know plenty. But I'd never heard of Jāzeps until yesterday.

Right?

In my head, I flip through my memories of all the places we've traveled, all the people we've met. No, no, and no. Not one person named Jāzeps. It's a strange enough name that I would've remembered if I'd met someone with it.

But I do remember something else going through my memories. When Miriam was born, a man came to visit us. He was an older, shrunken man with a beard of wispy white hair. He'd come in like a Hebraic Santa Claus with a knapsack of presents dangling from his hand: a kosher cookbook for my mother, fancy combs for my hair, a leather-bound Torah for my dad. I don't remember much about his visit, still in a sleepless fog from helping my mom with Miriam, except that he was so happy. His eyes twinkled, and he bounced on feet so little that they looked like they belonged to an elf.

"Call me Joe," he'd said as he beamed at me.

I never saw him again although, every once in a while, my dad and Dr. Elías would mention him. They never said more than say they needed to contact him, and neither had any emotion, positive or negative, the few times he did come up. I never thought about it, just assumed he was a faraway scholar in Israel that they occasionally posed a question to.

"Is there a picture of Jāzeps?" I ask.

Angelina keys a few things into the laptop and then spins it to me. "Does he look familiar?"

I study the grainy, out-of-focus, black-and-white picture. Black dots swarm in front of my eyes as I grip the table in front of me.

Breathe, I tell myself.

But I can't. The black dots crowd together to form an impenetrable wall as my lungs collapse.

Bowie runs toward me, his arms outstretched. "I've got you" is the last thing I hear before I collapse.

I awake in Bowie's arms, Angelina dabbing my brow with a wet cloth.

"That was quite the scare you gave us," she says.

Bowie squeezes me to him as my hair streams down his chest.

"I've never heard of Jāzeps," I say. "But the man in that picture may be a person—make that the only person—who visited us when Miriam was born."

"What did he do while he visited?" he asks.

"Handed out presents, had a private discussion with Dr. Elías and my dad. He left before dinner."

"Have you seen him since?" Angelina probes.

I shake my head. "My dad and Dr. Elías would mention him from time to time, but it was usually in passing." I shrug. "I always assumed he was a religious scholar who they posed theological questions to." I hesitate, thinking more about the conversations I'd overheard about Jāzeps. "I always thought he was based in Israel since, a couple of times, Dr. Elías and my dad had questions about the Third Temple, which will be built when the Mashiach ben David comes."

"You've had a tail for years, courtesy of Jāzeps. Our guest yesterday was the latest." Angelina flips a braid over her shoulder.

"And probably the weakest." She smirks. "One really shouldn't try to save a few quid when hiring a hitman."

My jaw drops. "A hitman?"

"For us," Angelina says. "We were the targets, not you."

"Why?"

"That's what we're trying to figure out," Bowie says. "All we know is that yesterday's poor excuse for an assassin was supposed to bring you back to Jāzeps unharmed. If we became fish food, then that was the cost of doing business."

"Where is he now?" I ask, more curious than caring.

"Fish food, darling. Jāzeps got rid of him last night after he came back empty-handed with his sad, sad story of how mean Bowie had been to him.

I slump against Bowie's chest, too overwhelmed to stand up on my own.

"I've still got you, Snow White," he whispers. My body goes filmy as he brushes a kiss against my hair.

Angelina snaps her fingers. "This is a thriller, not a rom-com. Stay focused."

"Focused on what?" I ask. "What am I going to do?"

"That, darling, is a question for tomorrow."

"Why?" I rub my hands together. If all of this is real, then I want to take action immediately. To do what, I don't know, but I would guess that Bowie and Angelina have some ideas.

"I'm leaving. My apartment has been deemed safe."

"Really?"

"The man in tan snatched me only a block away from Bowie's." She rolls her eyes. "A good criminal would have followed me home and then grabbed me when I left again. But this lad was in such a hurry. Anyway, a member of the Pact will meet me, disguise me, and then whisk me home." She arches an eyebrow. "Not that this hasn't been lovely, cooped up with a pair of lovebirds while eating bowls of salt and sugar."

"Where do you live?" I ask, curious about how someone like

Angelina lives in plain sight. Between the beauty and the accent, she's way too memorable to blend in just anywhere.

I glance at Bowie, who is sitting in a chair, his hoodie hanging low over his face.

Maybe it's easier than I think. Because I can't imagine Bowie hiding in plain sight, and that's exactly what's he done for two years in New York.

"Or maybe you can't tell me," I say.

Angelina's haughty expression relaxes, and she flashes a rare smile. I wouldn't put money on it, but I think she's come around to me.

"I don't live in Queens," she says. "I can tell you that much."

I wave as she prances out of the door, swinging her braids over a shoulder as she goes.

I turn to Bowie with a bright expression. "More ramen or sardines and crackers. You pick." The ends of my stomach point down at both of these options.

"No, and definitely no. We're ordering in." He reaches for his phone. "What can you eat again?"

"Everything."

His hand relaxes around the phone. "Everything?"

I nod. "I've had enough of rules for the time being. I want a hamburger."

"Your wish," he taps a few things into his phone, "is my command."

"How are you going to manage delivery when we're in a high-security tower?"

He blows me a kiss. "Back in five, Snow White."

And he is, bringing in a bag that smells of the formula to American culinary happiness: meat + bread.

"How did the delivery guy get past security?" I ask as I pull out plates and napkins.

I've only been here a day, but I've got our "safe-ment" protocol down. Safe-ment is my silly portmanteau for our safe house that's also an apartment. I learned the word portmanteau from a half-filled crossword puzzle I'd ripped out of a magazine I'd found in a Dallas coffee shop.

Bowie unwraps our burgers and places them on our plates. "He didn't get past security. I met him before the doorman could call up."

I take a bite. The umami-salt-fat trifecta hits my tongue, and I murmur in delight.

Bowie looks up from his burger. "You like it?"

I point to my burger, which is already half-eaten. "You think?"

He leans across the table and gives me an easy kiss. It should be a nothing kiss although it's anything but. This is the type of kiss husbands give wives when they pass each other in the hall, one carrying a sleepy child to bed, the other bringing folded laundry to put away.

It is the kiss of every day, of enjoying your beloved in the hurricane of work and family.

It is the kiss Bowie and I will never truly share since the last grain of sand runs out on our relationship in just a few days.

Remembering my decision, I park this thought. Instead, I ask Bowie about his apartment. "Will you be able to go back to your home?"

He ducks his head as he reaches for a fry but not before I catch his drawn brows and empty eyes.

"No."

"Will you miss it?" I ask after savoring the last bite of my burger.

He nods. "It became home as much as any place can in my line of work." He pauses. "I always thought I was a country boy, but I've enjoyed city life. I like getting pizza at midnight or going for a jog early in the morning and waving hello to my neighbors." He scowls but then brightens a little. "They got my coffee cups out, so I'll be able to keep those."

"Are you going to a state where you'll be able to get a new cup?"

He shrugs. "After everything that's happened, the Pact will probably station me on the other side of the world."

"Oh." I look down at my empty plate. Even though I know I won't see Bowie again in a few days, I always imagined him being closer.

"I broke the rules big time here," he says.

"Are they punishing you?"

Bowie shakes head. "They're protecting me." He points at me. "You too."

21

B owie and Angelina sit me down the next morning to tell it to me straight. Their faces are taut with worry.

"You're in a heap of trouble, darling," Angelina says as she leans forward, her braids falling over her shoulders. "Your family is connected to one of the most notorious criminals working today. Jāzeps is frantically trying to find you. To do what with, we don't know. I, however, imagine it's nothing pleasant."

"What makes Jāzeps so notorious?" I ask.

"He's a craftsman," Angelina says. "He builds disgusting chatrooms and depraved websites as a way to get people into his lair. Once they're there, he encourages them to linger, to make themselves comfortable with more gross enticements at a very low price. As soon as they try to leave, he demands an exit fee."

"Why?"

Bowie scowls. "Because, otherwise, he'll notify the friends, families, and employers about the visitor's vice. He's the worst kind of criminal, making money on the front end and back end."

"Oh." Although I go for confidence, the word wobbles like a glass about to break, which is pretty much how I feel.

Angelina says, "We're not sugarcoating it, darling. We want you to know the truth so that you can make the best decision for yourself."

"Not to scare you too much," Bowie says, "but you're in danger. If you want to get away from him, the Pact can get you into a new identity by the beginning of next week. They can even get you into a Jewish community if that's what you want, or they can set you up as a college student in a small town." He gazes deep into my eyes. "You'll be safe, but the safety comes with a price."

"What price is that?" I ask.

"You'll need to lie low for a couple of years. You can't see your family. You can't even contact them. When the coast is clear, maybe." His voice goes low and dark. "But we're dealing with a guy like Jāzeps, which means the coast might never be clear."

I try to imagine what that would be like, moving to a new town by myself, never seeing my family again, having no one who would know the real me.

It would be like Bowie's life.

I shake my head. I might be safe, but I would be living a lie. Plus, I can't abandon Miriam until she's safe.

"I want to go back to my family," I say. "I have to."

Bowie and Angelina exchange looks.

"While that is an admirable choice, it is also a foolhardy one," Angelina says.

"I know. But I couldn't live with myself if I did anything else."

Bowie reaches across the table and squeezes my hand. Tears prick in my eyes at how comforted I am by his warm, strong grip. I push them back as he half-smiles at me with tender eyes.

Angelina rolls her eyes. "Stop mooning over each other. We've got work to do."

"What kind of work?" I ask.

Angelina pushes a laptop across the table at me. "I'm going to teach you how to hack."

Bowie reaches into his hoodie and pulls out a small knife in a sheath. "And I'm going to teach you how to fight."

"Brains and brawn," Angelina says. "You must have both if you're going to have any chance."

"Why do I need to learn to hack?" I ask. "I know nothing about computers." I look at Angelina pleadingly. "Anyway, couldn't you hack into Dr. Elías' computer?"

Angelina folds her arms across her chest. "I can do no such thing. The Pact insists on evidence before I enter a private citizen's computer. Dr. Elías has a very faint footprint on the internet, which is to say he isn't active on any forums or social media. Besides email and banking, he rarely uses the internet."

"That's because he's not allowed to. Rabbis consider the internet to be a great spiritual danger. So . . . couldn't you try, considering how little there probably is?"

"Darling, do you think Dr. Elías is part of this cockamamie scheme to bring the Mashiach ben David for noble reasons or self-interested ones?"

I run my hands through my hair. "I . . . don't know why he's part of it, to be honest."

I'd accepted Dr. Elías' explanation for so long that I hadn't bothered to question his motives. But they need to be questioned. Because Angelina is right. Dr. Elías must have a real reason hiding beyond the pretend one.

"It's probably not for noble reasons," I say.

"Precisely," Angelina says triumphantly. "Jāzeps has something on him, and," she fixes her eyes on me, "you are going to find it."

"But how? I haven't touched one in years."

She rolls her eyes at me. "Do you know what my experience was with computers before I started hanging out in an internet café?"

I shake my head.

"Not a single thing. I didn't even know how to turn one on, much to the everlasting mirth of the people there. If I can learn everything, then you can learn something."

She turns her gaze to the computer. "The basics first. You need to learn a few programming languages."

For what seems like a year but in reality is only a few hours, Angelina introduces me to various programming languages with names like video games: Python, Bash, and Assembly. My head is spinning by the time she draws her lecture to a close.

"Study," she says. "You have a lot to remember. This is a skill that you can use for the rest of your life, so learn it well." Angelina gives me a piercing look. "As with all things in life, remember that you will never be ready. The perfect moment will never arrive. Opportunities are made, not presented."

I hold my throbbing head in my hand as I munch on a quick lunch of crackers, beef jerky, and raisins. I'd like to fall asleep, but Bowie shows up and I perk up.

I smile at him, but he doesn't return it.

"Follow me," he says.

We do the old ride in the elevator to different floors before we get off at eleven. Bowie leads me into an apartment that has nothing: no furniture, no curtains, not even a speck of dust.

"On loan for the week," he says.

"Whose is it?" I ask. "And why don't they keep anything here?"

"I don't know who it belongs to, only that it's safe. As for nothing being here, I wouldn't be so sure about that."

I scan the room, my eyes catching on a closet. Has someone hidden jewels in it? Maybe stacks of cash rest under the floorboards. I start to fan myself in excitement.

Bowie guesses my thoughts. "Nothing like that, Snow White. This is probably the 'official' office for a shell company."

He sees my questioning look. "To keep from paying taxes. There's nothing rich people hate more than that."

My chest deflates as if it were a balloon Bowie has stepped on.

"I know, I know," he says. "It's so much more fun to imagine this place as an abandoned pirate ship, but the truth is much more ordinary." He stares at me, his sky-blue eyes hard with purpose. "Besides, you've got plenty of truth that's stranger than fiction to deal with right now."

"Like learning how to use a knife?"

"Like that." Then, before I can even process what he's doing, he's lobbing something at me. "Think fast," he says, but there's no thinking fast. As I extend my hands out to catch the thin, cylindrical object sailing through the air, he darts in front of me and grabs it. He turns to face me, a marker dangling from his hand.

"The thing about fighting with a knife is that you have to be faster and smarter than the guy with a gun. People are scared of a gun because it's a stupid weapon. Even an idiot can kill with it." He twirls the marker between his second and third fingers. "A knife, though, that's an intellectual's weapon."

"Really?" I ask. If I had to choose, I'd rather have a gun in a fight than a knife even if it is the idiot's weapon of choice. I don't care about being smart. I only care about staying alive.

"Drawing a weapon isn't about fighting, Hannah." He brandishes the marker. "It's about winning. Plenty of times, the other guy is going to have a bigger, better weapon than you. He will know more tricks than you. Your goal is to disarm him and then get away fast before he knows what happened. It's a magic trick."

I think back to what Angelina said about hacking. Magic seems to be the name of the game when it comes to beating a criminal enterprise.

"Listen, Hannah," Bowie says. "This is important. You're a woman. No one will expect anything from you beyond tears and submission. You could take anyone down simply because they'll never expect you to do so."

"I don't want to kill anyone," I say. "Please don't teach me that."

He smiles savagely. "I don't have to. You already saw how to do that when I killed Father O'Donnell."

I clutch my arms to my chest, my body weak and wavy.

That's right.

I'm here because I saw an assassination. And now the assassin is teaching me how to assassinate someone.

The world makes no sense.

22

B owie scoops me in his arms and presses me tight to him. "I'm not going to hurt you. Ever." He kisses the top of my head. "The truth is that I'd hurt for you."

I relax against him, feeling small and precious, like a pearl cradled in an oyster's shell.

"My word is my bond," he says, his tone dogged. "Remember that. Even if it's the only thing you remember."

"I know."

And I do know. Bowie has never once lied to me or pretended to be anything other than what he is. And, while I don't know everything about him and probably never will, I know he keeps his word.

He pulls away from me and stares deep into my eyes. "I want you to get out of whatever trouble you're in. And I want you to get Miriam out of it too." He hands me a marker. "For today, these are our knives." He half-smiles. "They're kids' markers, so they'll wash out of our clothes."

"Really?"

"You need to see where you're hitting and how clean the stroke is. I've taken out a lot of snakes in my career, but I've never been sloppy with them because they're bad. I might let them suffer for a minute or two to make sure they understand what's happening and why it's happening, but I'll never injure someone so that they spend hours in agony."

I nod although I'm not sure what to make of these ethics. I guess dying quickly is better than dying slowly, but regardless, it all ends the same.

"I'll learn how to wound someone. But I don't want to hurt anyone permanently." I say. "I know you kill. I saw you kill. But I can't. I just can't. It's not a judgment against you or what you do. But it is a judgment against me and what I can do."

"I appreciate your honesty." His eyes darken. "I won't teach you to kill. But if you don't want to kill, then stay away from the trunk of the body where the organs are." He taps my heart and stomach with the marker. "One stab is all it'll take."

"Okay," I say in a small voice.

"You need to know how to wound someone well enough so that it'll buy you enough time to get away and get help."

He drops to his knees and slices his marker across the backs of my heels. "Achilles' tendons are good. You can drop low before anyone realizes what's happened. Plus, even a bad job will buy you enough time to run away."

Then, before I even have time to process what's happening, he takes his marker and jabs it into my stomach.

"Bull's eye," he says, but there's no pride in it. "While you're deciding whether you're up to fighting or if you should run, that's how quickly the other guy will decide to kill you."

I gaze at the black splotch on my cherry red hoodie. Why did Bowie think I could ever do anything even close to what he does? I've never even raised a hand in anger to someone. How could I stab them, slice them and dice them?

"The first rule of self-defense is to always assume your attacker is armed. He—because it's almost always a he—will hurt you if he has to. He will be big; he will have friends; and he will attack you when you are alone and distracted. Most importantly, the fight is *never* over. Unless—"

"He's dead," I say for him.

"It's the only way to be sure."

Using the markers, Bowie takes me through the two basic grips: forward and reverse. I call them sky and ground based on the direction the blade is pointing. It takes me a while to get the hang of it. My fingers cramp, and I can't figure out where I want my thumb placed.

"When you fight," he says, "you play offense and defense at the same time."

"How do I do that?"

"The knife is to attack the perpetrator. It's also to protect yourself, so keep it near your face, neck, and shoulder. Then, make your body as small as possible."

Bowie demonstrates, somehow folding his enormous bulk in on itself, so he looks like a turtle hiding in his shell. I try to mimic him. It's harder than it appears, ducking my head but keeping my eyes up.

"Pretty good," he says. "Now, you've got to move. The more you stay in constant motion, the harder it will be for the perp to get you."

Like a boxer, I bounce on my toes, all the while keeping myself as small as possible. Bowie makes me practice until I'm panting and slick with sweat.

He takes the marker from me and then draws me close for a hug. "You did great today, Hannah."

"Thanks," I say as my cheeks heat up.

"Tomorrow, we'll learn how to strike with a knife. The day after that, we'll practice with a real knife." He drops a kiss on top of my head. "I'm moving faster than I'd like, but you have to be ready." He pauses. "For the worst because that might be how it goes down."

The rest of the week flies by. Each day, Angelina and Bowie add to my skills and refine what I've learned. As the days tick by, I find I like knife fighting more than I like hacking, which surprises me. Hacking is boring and frustrating with lots of failures before success comes out of nowhere. Although I've never gambled before, it feels like the two have a lot in common.

Fighting, on the other hand, has defined steps and concrete goals—to survive and, hopefully, disarm or disrupt your opponent. The first time I knock Bowie's knife out of his hand, he flashes me a huge smile that makes me flush with pride. The next day he gives me my own knife, one just like his except with a smaller, four-inch blade.

"Easier for you to hide," he says. "It's not practical to wear it all the time, but keep it within an arm's length distance." He finds my eyes. "Promise me."

"I promise."

Although he and Angelina have warned me over and over about the danger I'm in, my reasons for getting good only start with that. They end with the fact that I want to earn their respect. They may be on the wrong side of the law, but each of them has a code of ethics stronger and more thoughtful than plenty of people on the right side of the law.

I'll never be a professional like them, but I've come a long way. I can work my way into a bank account and out of chokehold. Along the way, I start to have a new respect for myself. I'd been given so little to do for so long that I'd forgotten how much I could do.

At night, Bowie and I eat dinner together, talking and telling stories. At night, we kiss for hours before falling asleep in each other's arms.

We haven't slept-slept together yet although all the kissing makes me want to. Really, really want to. I want to show Bowie how I feel on the inside.

Plus, even though I'm supposed to want to wait until I'm married, the idea of hanging out until then seems silly. A husband might never show up. And, even if he does, is that what he's going to care about when he finds out my secret? I didn't think so.

Bowie is the one holding back.

"I'm bad news," he says any time I let my hands drift down his chest, my fingers riding over the hard planes of his body.

The last night should have been a celebration. I'm going home to my family with a slew of new skills and self-respect to boot. Bowie has ordered a meal fit for royalty, complete with caviar, champagne, and steaks with truffle fries. At my insistence, Angelina stays.

She even offers a toast. "To Snow White, who showed us that fairy tale princesses are capable of more than singing songs to woodland creatures." She stares deep into my eyes. "May you remember that when you return home."

We clink glasses as I sniff. That means something coming from Angelina.

We try in vain to make conversation, but none of us has much to say beyond commenting on how delicious the food is. Bowie and I spend most of our time gazing at each other.

It will be impossible to remember everything, but I want to remember the most important thing—the happiness. I wasn't unhappy prior to meeting Bowie, but spending time with Angelina and him did point out all the ways I'd stopped growing as a person and how nice it is to spend time with people my own age.

I clear my throat and raise my glass. "Thank you," I say over the lump in my throat. "I know I've been an unconventional, unexpected guest, but you've done so much for me." I look down. "I appreciate it."

After the toast, Angelina rises and hugs me. "Be brave and be quick, darling."

After she leaves in rat-a-tat of swinging braids and clacking heels, my shoulders droop.

"I can't believe I'm about to say this, but I'm going to miss her."

Bowie laughs. "The feeling is mutual. You won her over, which is not easy to do."

I jump up and walk over to him. I swallow to steady my jumpy nerves as I extend my arm to him.

"Bowie," I whisper.

He turns my hand over and brushes a kiss over it. "What do you need?"

"You."

23

My cheeks get hot at how forward I am, how honest I'm being. I chalk it up to the champagne, which has made me feel bright and sparkly.

"Are you sure, Hannah? It's not something you can give again."

"I am." I hesitate. "But I have a request."

"What's that?"

"The lights . . . I want them off."

I don't want Bowie to see, to know, for the judgment that will follow. I don't want this act, which I want to be beautiful, to turn ugly.

So lights out is the only way it's going to happen.

"Is it a religious thing?" he asks.

I could lie and tell Bowie, yes, it has to do with my religion, which would be a sure-fire way to prevent questions. Instead, I keep with my practice of truth-telling.

"More of a me thing," I say, my arm still outstretched.

He takes my hand. "You're gorgeous, Hannah. Inside and out. "

I won't be if you see me naked, I think.

"I want to see you." His voice is low and urgent. "I want you to see me."

I shake my head. "Lights off."

"You drive a tough bargain, Snow White."

"Five minutes," I say before dashing into the bedroom.

Once there, I close the blinds tightly and slip out of my leggings and hoodie. I fluff my hair out and lie on the bed. The last thing I do is tap the lamp beside the bed, which is one of those fancy lights that flick on and off at the touch of a finger. The room snaps to black.

I fidget with the edge of the comforter. Should I get in bed or stay on top? I turn the question over in my mind, but I'm saved from answering it because the door is opening and Bowie is coming into the room. He's turned off the lights in the living room, so our entire world is dark.

He slides into bed and rolls until he is beside me. My heart thwacks against my chest. I know what's supposed to happen next, but I'm not sure if I should do something to get it started.

I open my mouth to say something, but Bowie kisses me, one of those slow-burn kisses where the heat unfurls down my body like a fiery streamer. My toes curl, and I arch my back.

Without removing his lips, he takes a hand and begins to explore my body. He finds areas—earlobes, the underside of my chin, the inside of my arms—that I had no idea are so sensitive. Beneath his fingers, I twitch and moan.

Maybe I should be embarrassed by my lack of modesty, but I'm not. I feel like I'm coming to life.

Bowie dips his head and nudges it in between my legs. With his tongue, he finds my small, tender nub. He—so slowly—swirls his tongue around it as I begin to pulse. Incrementally, he increases the pressure and tempo as my breath flees.

Then, like a newly lit firecracker, the heat surges through me until it can't be contained anymore. I explode into stardust, all silvery flashes and shiny fragments.

Drifting through outer space is so wonderful that it takes some time for me to alight to earth again. Finally, I open my eyes and inhale. I feel boneless, as if my insides were liquid gold. Bowie holds me close as I melt into him. This time, I initiate the kiss.

Gently, he lays me down, his body overwhelming me with its heat and hardness.

I can't wait for him to be inside me.

"Last chance to back out," he says, the words snarled with desire. "And just for the record, I'm happy with whatever you're happy with."

I don't answer. Instead, I wrap my legs around his waist. He takes his time, breaching me, filling me, reaching into the deepest part of me. It takes a minute for me to adjust his overwhelming presence, but I do. Following my instinct, I tilt my pelvis to him, inviting him to go even further.

Groaning, he does, and we begin to move together. The intensity—unexpected but welcome—builds and builds until I become stardust again.

So caught up in my own bliss that I don't realize Bowie has left me. A blister-hot liquid gushes beside me. He collapses against my chest, our frantic hearts thumping against each other.

"I should have used something, but I had to be skin to skin with you. I wasn't going to be a jerk, though, and leave you with a potential problem, seeing as I'll be on the other side of the world in a day or so." He rolls off me and starts pawing around on the nightstand. "Let me get a tissue."

I'm trying to process what Bowie is telling me, so I don't realize that he's accidentally brushed the light, its golden glow spilling around the room, illuminating exactly what I don't want Bowie to see.

He turns his head, his mouth forming the word *sorry*. Then, his eyes widen as he processes the improbability of the blood on my thighs and the scar stretching across my abdomen.

Too late, I pull the sheet over my stomach, but it doesn't matter.

"Tell me, Hannah spelled the same way going forward as backward, how are you a virgin with a C-section scar?"

I consider lying, telling Bowie that I had lady troubles and had to have an operation.

I don't.

If I couldn't lie before I knew Bowie, then there's no way I could lie now. Plus, I want to tell someone who isn't part of Dr. Elías' harebrained scheme. I want outside validation that it was wrong, that it will be wrong when it happens to Miriam.

Bowie waits, his body rigid.

I close my eyes, knowing that as soon as I tell Bowie, he will reject me, his Snow White permanently blemished.

It's okay, I think. *It's not like you were going to see him again after tonight. He can file our romance as some fling he had with a weird, broken girl.*

As for me, I'll look forward to nursing a broken heart.

"Were you a true virgin?"

I nod.

"Is that a C-section scar?"

I nod again.

"What happened?" He refuses to look at me. "Tell me."

I gulp.

Breathe, I tell myself.

In a tiny, tight voice, I say, "Miriam isn't my sister. She's my daughter."

"How old is Miriam?"

"She turned fourteen in early September."

"So you're . . ."

"Twenty-eight."

Bowie swears before punching the mattress. Startled, I leap out of bed, clutching the sheet to me as tears spurt down my cheeks.

"I'm sorry," I say. "I know it's horrifying."

Bowie turns to me, his face tense with anger. "Who did that to you?"

"Dr. Elías," I whisper. "This is part of his plan."

"Impregnating a fourteen-year-old girl is part of his plan? That's insane," Bowie yells.

He is a truly terrifying sight when angry, his enormous body quivering, the veins roping his arms standing up. I back away to the door, holding the sheet away from me, like it's a white flag of surrender.

He drops his head into his hands. "I'm sorry. I got carried away because I'm angrier than I have been in years."

"I'm sorry," I say again.

"You're sorry?" Bowie laughs incredulously. "You have nothing to be sorry for." He looks at me, a vein pulsing in his forehead. "The people who did this you? They should be sorry. Very sorry."

"Maybe," I say as I lean against the door to push it open. I don't want to talk anymore.

"Hannah, wait. Tell me why Dr. Elías did this to you." Under his breath, he mutters, "So I can decide how sorry I'd like to make him."

I don't do or say anything, just stare at him as my heart thumps against my chest.

Bowie walks over and takes the sheet from my shaking hands. He tosses it on the bed and then pulls me close. With his big, warm hands, he rubs my back.

"Tell me," he says. "So I can make it better."

BOWIE HAS STATIONED me on the sofa, a steaming cup of herbal tea in my hands. He uses his body like a blanket, covering me and protecting me.

I take a sip of the tea, trying to figure out how to explain Dr. Elías' plan. The whole thing doesn't make total sense to me, so I can't imagine it's going to be any clearer to Bowie.

"What do you know about the Immaculate Conception?" I ask, just to start the conversation somewhere.

He scratches his head. "It's when Mary—"

"Miriam," I say. "That's the Hebrew version of Mary."

"I didn't know that."

I gesture to the window where, outside, a twinkling landscape of lights unspools. "You and probably plenty of the world. Mary would have been a Jewish girl."

"So the Immaculate Conception is the virgin birth."

I shake my head. "Wrong, and the Catholic Church is very clear on this. The Immaculate Conception is the idea that Miriam is born without sin. The virgin birth is when Miriam gives birth to Yeshua."

"Really?"

"Really," I say.

"How does that fit in with everything?"

"I am directly descended from Nathan, a son of King David." I answer Bowie's questioning look. "Dr. Elías tested my family's DNA." I shrug. "Anyway, it was all there. I could be the mother of Miriam if he could figure out how to get her born without sin."

Bowie keeps his voice even, but his body tightens up when he asks, "Then what?"

"I give birth to Miriam. Miriam gives birth to the Mashiach ben David after being married to and artificially inseminated by a man who is descended from both David and Solomon. The Jewish people come back to Israel to enjoy a thousand years of peace and prosperity."

He frowns in confusion. "But the Jewish people don't believe that Jesus was the Messiah. Why is Dr. Elías trying to recreate the circumstances of Jesus's birth?'

"That," I say, "has to do with a major disagreement between the Christian and Jewish faiths regarding how the Hebrew word *almah* should be translated."

"What does it mean?"

"The Jewish people believe it refers to a girl who has gone through puberty. Christians, though, believe it means a *virgin* who has gone through puberty."

"That's a big difference."

I take a sip of tea as I organize my thoughts. "Dr. Elías grew in the Catholic church where the virgin birth is its very foundation. He literally couldn't accept the idea that the Mashiach ben David would be born in and of sin. So he came up with the idea that would allow Miriam's son to be conceived of and born by a virgin." I hesitate. "He also thinks that's why the Jewish people are still waiting, no matter how awful things have been for them."

"Because he would have been conceived the normal way?" Bowie's brow wrinkles. "Swiss cheese has fewer holes than this."

"It sounds crazy, but Dr. Elías has studied the book of Isaiah extensively, and he is convinced that the only way for the Mashiach ben David to come, and believed as such, is for him to be born of a virgin."

"Why use you, a fourteen-year-old girl? Why not find someone older with a similar lineage?"

I sigh. "*Almahs* with my lineage are few and far between. Anyway, in the Christian New Testament, Miriam was likely around my age when she gave birth to Yeshua."

Bowie shakes his head, his eyes closed. "It's hard for me to wrap my head around this."

"I know," I say. "I've been living it for years and years, so I've had lots of practice wrapping my head around it. But, if you spent any time reading the Tanakh—that's the Hebrew Bible—or the

Christian Bible, this isn't any crazier than Moses parting the Red Sea or Elisha's bones reviving the dead."

"And the purpose of this is to keep the Jewish people from getting persecuted again?"

I nod. "Dr. Elías hoped that, if nothing else, it would spark an exodus of the Jewish people."

"They all go to Israel?"

"Quickly and with purpose because they know the timeline."

"What timeline is that?"

"The Jewish prophecy states that the Mashiach ben David must come before the year 6,000, which is two centuries and some change away."

"Why 6,000 years?"

"Each millennium stands for one day of the week. For six days, you work. On the seventh day, you rest. The six millennia of creation that have passed will end in the sanctified seventh millennia."

"In other words, time's running out?"

"Pretty much. Plus, for the first time in the history of humanity, we have DNA testing and in vitro fertilization to make the miracle a reality."

"Your parents believe this?"

I nod. "They believe their struggles led them to Dr. Elías. That we were shown great favor by HaShem to help usher in the Messianic era."

I catch Bowie's confused look. "We don't use the name of . . ." I hunt for a term that he'll understand. "The big guy in the sky."

"You don't?"

"It consists of four vowels, and it's considered to be a powerful thing, so we made up these other words like Yahweh and HaShem."

"One thing I know for sure is that Dr. Elías is a flunky," Bowie says. "This is Jāzeps's plan. The time, the money, the sick obsession that clouds all reason. Only a top-drawer criminal could come up with that. Dr. Elías is just taking orders."

"But why is Jāzeps doing this?" I ask. "Even if he sees it all the way through, there's no guarantee he's going to save the Jewish people. There are way too many variables to control, even if people believe him and Miriam's child ends up being better than ordinary."

He rubs my cheek. "People like Jāzeps and—I've got to tell it like it is—the billionaires I work for, they aren't like us. They don't care about risks or drawbacks, which isn't the same thing as taking care to manage risk and avoid drawbacks. They see the reward, the hard work, and the patience needed to earn that reward. That's why plenty of them started from nothing and worked their way up until they became someone. They had a dream, and they wouldn't let anyone tell them it wouldn't work. They do crazy things just because they can."

"Just because they can?"

I finish my tea and put the cup on an end table, regretting even the several seconds that I have to peel my body away from Bowie.

He nods. "The Pact is a crazy idea. So is Jāzeps's plan. But when you have money, that kind of crazy can be papered over with dollar bills."

"I've got the thumb drive Angelina gave me," I say. "I'm going to find the connection between Dr. Elías and Jāzeps."

Bowie pulls me close. "I know you will."

I relax against him, letting his strong arms bring me closer.

"I have to ask. Why did your parents let you have a baby at fourteen?"

"Because girls had babies at fourteen back then."

"I'm not a woman, but I know having a baby at that age isn't a good idea for a lot of reasons."

I shrug. "Times were different. At twelve, a girl became a woman and was able to be betrothed. After that, if a girl had menstruated, then she was old enough to be a mother. Dr. Elías believes if women were supposed to wait to have babies, then HaShem would have delayed puberty for girls. Instead, today, plenty of girls get their periods earlier than ever. Dr. Elías says it's a sign that girls should return to marrying and having children when their bodies tell them they're ready to do so."

"Dr. Elías is full of crap," Bowie says. "Women didn't have many choices back then. Now they do." He laughs without humor. "Thanks to all the advances in science that will allow a virgin to give birth."

I nod. "Miriam was made in a Petri dish and implanted in me using the sperm of a Jewish man with the ideal lineage. All I know is his name was Joachim." I smile ruefully. "It took a couple of tries to get me pregnant. That got Dr. Elías excited. He said I was just like Miriam's mom, Hannah, who Christians know as Saint Anne. She had fertility troubles."

"Were you married?" He pauses. "That's how it had to be, right?"

"Yes, although I never met him. He was old and infirm and had the good manners to die when Miriam was a baby."

His jaw drops. "What . . ."

"It sounds crazy. It is crazy in today's time. But for thousands of years, girls were married off to old men after they had their periods. It's written everywhere throughout history."

I look out the window, the city darkening, light by light turning off, as people go to sleep. "I consider myself lucky. If I'd been born a couple of hundred years earlier, then I probably would have been married off to an old man before dying in childbirth."

Bowie squeezes me. "I'm not so naïve to think that barely teenagers don't have babies these days, but it's hard to understand it happening so methodically and with so much adult enthusiasm."

I think for a minute about that time. "We were isolated," I say. "My parents were ashamed when everything happened. They wouldn't contact family, and they cut off their friends. They wouldn't even step into the Reform temple we'd gone to on and off for years because they couldn't take the humiliation. Dr. Elías was the first person they had to talk to in a long time. I think they were desperate to have purpose restored to their lives."

"Did you have an okay birth?"

"I carried Miriam until she was 37 weeks and then had a C-section. The doctor wouldn't let me go until my due date since pregnancy at that age is very risky." In a small voice, I say, "So now you why I was a virgin with a C-section scar."

Bowie falls silent. I'm not sure if he wants to hear anymore, so I get quiet myself.

"How was it?" he asks. "Being pregnant at such a young age."

"We were in Mexico—that's the only place they could find a doctor who would do it—in a town near the beach. I spent my days swimming in a pool with turquoise water and eating quesadillas squeezed with fresh limes. Everybody loved me and petted me and cared about my welfare." I hesitate. "It was still close to the awful time that it felt like a small sacrifice for everyone to be happy again."

"What happened after the delivery?"

"They told me Miriam would be my sister from here on out. I was young and confused and in pain, so I didn't know what else to do except follow directions. After recovering for a couple of months, we hit the road."

Bowie kisses the top of my head. "I'm sorry this happened to you."

"Me too, but I don't care about the past anymore. I care about the future."

"Miriam's future?"

I nod. "She's already thirteen, and her first period started last week. That's why I was in the church that day at that time. I had to do something before something is done to her."

"What were you really going to ask the priest?"

"I wanted to find out why the Catholic church translates *almah* one way and the Jewish people another. I wanted to ask if the church believes that the Miriam in their Bible was barely a teenager when she gave birth. I wanted to ask what would happen if the Mashiach ben David did come because, it seems to me, at least, that a lot of non-Jewish people might have strong opinions about it. Opinions they might act upon. Maybe even with violence." I hesitate for a moment. "But most of all, I wanted to know if it's as wrong as I think it is."

He strokes my hair. "You've been through a lot."

"Dr. Elías and Jāzeps aren't the first people to twist religion to suit their purpose." I look down at my hands. "For the longest time, I never thought of Miriam as my daughter. But when it became clear that what had been talked about in the abstract was going to become a reality, something primal in me snapped. It was like I'd been going through life in a fog, but then I woke up. I had to save her. If I didn't, I would have failed at the most basic act of motherhood—keeping my daughter safe."

I lift my hands in the air. "But I didn't have any good ideas, and, even if I did, I didn't have any resources to execute them."

"Does Miriam know what's going to happen?"

"She knows." I struggle to get the next words out of me. "The worst part is that she wants to go through with it."

Bowie's eyebrows shoot up. "She does?"

"Since the day she was born, she's been told this is her purpose in life. Plus, she's exactly the way you would imagine her to be. She's quiet, kind, perfect in her devotion."

"Is it going to be another in vitro fertilization and C-section?"

I nod. "Another virgin birth."

"Where is this taking place?"

I press my lips together. "We're not going to Mexico. Dr. Elías has found a doctor who will do it near here. Then, we leave for Jerusalem."

"And you're going to try to stop it?"

I sit up tall. "If it's the last thing I do."

In response, Bowie kisses me.

I don't sleep that night. Neither does Bowie. Instead, we cling to each other, all the lights blazing in the bedroom. There's no point in darkness. We know each other. The best thing we can do now is to see each other. We press our scars to each other, making a fence out of our pasts that don't push apart but instead draw us closer together.

I make a mental map of Bowie, memorizing every vein that threads through his arm, the way his hair curls a little at the nape of his neck. I'll never see him after tomorrow, but he'll live inside me for the rest of my life.

When the sun streams in the apartment, I shift myself until I'm on top of Bowie.

"One more time," I whisper. "So I can remember."

And he gives me something to remember by letting me take the lead. Although I'm shy at first, I rapidly become a fan of being on top. I vary my tempo: slow and quick and then slow again. I slant my body toward Bowie until my hair drifts around us like a black curtain. I arch backward. Sometimes, I sit upright, so I can watch his face, which is admiring and then smoldering.

I would keep going, but I can't. The pleasure is building to the point where I have to let go. Forgetting that I'm in a high-security building where I'm supposed to be discreet, I scream. Bowie—ever the gentleman by waiting for me—joins me, and our screams combine into an intense, emotional aria.

Panting, I collapse against him. He latches his arms around me and presses me so deep into him that it feels like I might dissolve into him.

"You do something to me, Hannah. Something no one else has ever done."

My heart flutters before freezing. I don't know how I'm going to pick up with my previous life and act like this never happened.

"What am I supposed to tell my family?" I ask suddenly.

He brushes a lock of hair out of my eyes. "The truth. As much or as little as you want."

"Why?"

"Because I'll be a new person with nothing in common with the old me by the time someone comes looking."

I nod as I change into the clothes I was wearing when I walked into the church to ask a question that I already knew the answer to.

"What happens next?" I ask.

"I kiss you good-bye, and then you walk out of here alone. After that, it's all up to you."

"Okay . . ." I say.

"One thing, though. The Pact is going to keep an eye on you until we figure out what the connection is between you, Jāzeps, and Dr. Elías."

He half-smiles at me. "With you on the inside, that may be sooner rather than the later." His lips flatten to a frown. "But anything could happen. Anything will happen. If you get into trouble, get yourself outside and look for a guy in a navy blue hoodie. Ask him what kind of pizza he likes."

"And then what?"

"Wait for his answer. If he says, 'sausage,' then go with him. He'll get you to safety." He gazes at me, his sky-blue eyes hard like marbles. "Do you understand?"

I nod as I run through the scenario in my head.

Bowie kisses me. "For the record, this has been one of the best weeks of my life."

I kiss him back. "Me too."

He pulls away. "Take care of yourself, Hannah."

"You too," I say as I edge toward the door. With my eyes on Bowie, I pull the door open and leave.

But only with my body.

My heart remains with him.

The first few minutes with my family are everything I've been dreaming they would be: hugs, kisses, tears, Salome wrapping her arms around my legs and squeezing me tight.

I forget the strange and wonderful week I had in the welcome embrace of my family.

Then the questions start.

I've decided to be as honest as possible. To tell the truth no matter what.

"Out of here," Dad says to Salome and Miriam. "Mom and I need to speak to Hannah alone." He waits for them to leave before turning to face me, his expression grave. "Where were you?"

"Did you hear about the assassination of Father O'Donnell?"

He nods as my mom looks confused. She doesn't pay attention to much of anything that doesn't have to do with family or faith.

"I was there."

Almost comically, their jaws drop open at the same time.

"I didn't do it."

"Obviously," Dad says.

I study him for a moment. He looks the same. His brown eyes wink owl-like behind a pair of silver glasses as his thinning hair wisps up and around his kippah.

"Yes, obviously," I say, going for a convincing tone. "I saw an assassin stab Father O'Donnell in the heart."

"What were you doing at a church of all places?" Dad asks.

"I went to ask the priest a question."

"What kind of a question?"

"I, um, I wanted to get the Catholic perspective of the virgin birth."

"Why?" Mom pipes in. "You could ask Dr. Elías."

I shift my gaze to her. She looks different even though it's only been a week since I've seen her. She's shrunk, her bones poking through parchment skin, her nose thinner and more prominent. She seems old, like a mama bird about to settle down for her final roost.

Although she hasn't said anything yet, her Graves' disease must be acting up. Maintaining her health is a balancing act. She tries to take good care of herself. Even with the stress my family has been under, she always goes to sleep early. But her anxiety flares in a second these days, and it must have been sky-high with me being missing for a week.

I bite my lip. While I'd been having a wonderful time with Bowie and Angelina, Mom had been suffering.

"Answer your mother's question, Hannah. Why didn't you ask Dr. Elías? He knows everything."

I stop myself just in time from rolling my eyes. Dr. Elías most certainly did not know everything.

Dad stares at me, unblinking through his glasses as he taps his foot.

I sigh. I'm going all in.

"I don't want Miriam to go through what I went through." I stand tall. "It isn't right."

Mom tut-tuts. "You're clearly upset by your ordeal." She leads me to the sofa, stiff and covered in ugly cabbage roses. I position myself on the edge as the plastic cover crinkles.

"Mom. It's true. A fourteen-year-old girl shouldn't have a baby because one guy—*one guy*—thinks he's figured out how to bring the Mashiach ben David, who, conveniently hasn't appeared in the thousands of years that he's been prophesied to appear."

I sweep my eyes over my parents and then wish I hadn't. Dad is glaring at me while Mom has slumped back into the sofa, her face pale.

"What did they do to you, Hannah?" Dad asks as Mom continues to lie on the sofa. "Where did they take you?"

"The assassin—I don't know his name—caught me. So he took me to his home." Behind my back, I touch the blade through my skirt. "He was . . . nice, surprisingly so. He cooked for me and gave me his bedroom."

Dad laughs like he doesn't believe me. "The assassin—the person who murdered another person in cold blood—was a good guy? Listen to yourself." He imitates my tone. "He was nice, surprisingly so. He cooked for me and gave me his bedroom."

I close my eyes. They don't believe me. Listening to myself talk, I wonder if it happened or if I just dreamed it.

I call up my memories of Bowie: the press of his lips, the touch of his hand, the architecture of his body that I leaned against so many times.

Then, I look at Dad, his arms folded across his chest, and Mom, still lying on the sofa, her skin pale and shiny.

Under my skin, my muscles jump. My parents are hopeless. I could tell them the whole truth and nothing but the truth, yet they wouldn't believe me. Their beliefs are such a part of them that they wouldn't even know who they are without it.

I close my eyes as I frantically think of what to say. Do I tell them I know about Jāzeps? Maybe that would shake them up enough for us to have an honest conversation.

I toss that idea out. They're not interested in anything honest, which means I need to lie to my parents to buy myself time until I figure out how to keep Miriam from becoming the next version of me. I take a deep breath and go for it.

"I met a guy, and I followed him to Brooklyn." Under my skirt, I cross my fingers. I haven't thought this story through, so I'm winging it.

"Where did you meet him?"

"A couple of weeks ago, when I took Salome to the park. We started talking, and it was fun. He was fun." I lift my chin high. "I never get to talk to people my own age. I'm lonely."

Although neither of them budges, my parents' eyes find each other.

"Nobody has cared about me since Miriam was born," I whine. "I'm tired of cleaning and cooking and taking care of kids all the time. I want more from life."

Inside, I preen. I'm pretty sure I'm doing a pretty good imitation of a put-upon teenager even though I'm technically a few years past this.

"What happened with the boy?" Dad asks.

"He invited me to a party." I bury my face in my hands. Not because I feel guilty about anything I'm saying, but because there's a high chance my face will give me away. "I waited until everyone went to bed and then snuck out."

I pretend to cry for a few minutes, and then I actually start to cry. The fact that neither of them has figured out I'm lying shines the truth hard into my eyes. I'm invisible to them beyond a pair of extra hands.

"Anyway, I went to his party, and he put me up with his sister's family, but then he dumped me this morning. He said I was a prude."

I spread my fingers and peek at my parents. They're having one of those silent conversations people who've been married for years have.

"That is entirely inappropriate behavior," Dad says. "A boy? Sneaking out? I'm disappointed in you, Hannah. I thought you were better than that."

"What good is 'being better than that' doing for me? I'm a spinster at twenty-eight with no husband, no children, and no life of my own."

I pull back the yarn a little. In my desire to spin a good lie, I might be spreading the manure too thick.

Mom wraps an arm around me. "One day, Hannah, you will have a husband and children of your own." She pulls away. "But first, we have to fulfill our destiny to save our people. To do that, we have to work together. You must be patient and accept that there are things bigger and more important than you."

At that moment, I fully accept the truth. My parents are brainwashed. We are part of a cult, a small, unusual one, but a cult nonetheless. They believe—would continue to believe—even in the face of evidence. They will go down with this ship, protesting that their truth is the only truth even as the lies swallow them whole.

The tears continue to flow faster and hotter down my cheeks as I realize that it comes down to me to get us out of this mess.

Through my tears, I gaze up at my parents, whose faces are set. The weight crashes down on my shoulders as I shudder.

At everything that is to come.

At everything that has come.

And at everything that will not come, which is Bowie, who is on his way to a place so far away from me that it might as well be the moon.

The day is long, longer than I remember it being, filled with cooking and cleaning and taking care of Salome, who is acting clingy. She circles her arms around my legs and weeps when I'm more than a few inches from her.

"Your sister missed you," Dad says at one point as I try to coax Salome into playing with a doll, so I can finish setting the table. He doesn't say the rest out loud, but his pointed look gives it away. *Your baby sister is traumatized because you decided to go gallivanting after a boy.*

I flush, but it's not because I'm embarrassed. I'm angry.

Salome was a surprise to everyone, most of all Mom, who thought she was long past the age of having children. She was so fatigued from the pregnancy and birth that it fell to me to take care of Salome. Although Salome knows I'm her sister, she treats me like her mother, mainly because I do the bulk of mothering for her.

I guess it's ironic. Miriam, my actual daughter, thinks of me as her sister while Salome, my sister, thinks of me as her mother. I love Salome, I do. But she's also why I'm stuck here. Without Salome, my parents might have encouraged me to get married and start my own family. I might not have had a lot of choices as far as suitors go, but someone would have come along who could have gone along with everything.

And then I never would have met Bowie, which causes my heart to ache. Although we weren't together for very long, he's left his handprint on my heart.

I push these thoughts from my head. Should've, would've, could've are useless right now as Salome is walking to me, her arms outstretched.

"Hug," she says. "Now." Covering my sigh with a smile, I hoist her up. She wraps her chubby legs around me and giggles into my hair.

It would be sweet if I weren't fixated on someone else.

Not Bowie although he isn't far from my thoughts.

Miriam.

I settle into my chair and place Salome next to me in preparation for the Shabbat dinner. Through the candlelight, I watch my daughter, trying to see her for the first time in a long time.

She looks the way you imagine she should look. Thick dark hair crests down her back, and her eyes shine with kindness. Technically, she's a woman a year gone, and her first menstrual cycle now ended. The bud is blooming with gentle curves and a small pimple on her chin, even though she still seems so young to me.

Miriam is the most naturally nice person I've come across, which isn't saying much since I don't know that many people. Even still, her niceness is undeniable. Tonight, at Shabbat dinner, she helps my mother bring the plates to the table. She wheedles Salome into eating a few bites of fish, so I can eat too. She stays reverent through the prayers and blessings.

As the courses progress, I get more and more suspicious, chewing the inside of my cheek. Maybe it's having been away from her for a week, something that's never happened, but something suddenly seems off about Miriam. She seems almost two-dimensional, like she's a paper doll.

It takes some time before I put my finger on it. Miriam doesn't appear to have an inner life with a conflict between her head and her heart. All the humor and self-reflection have been squeezed out of her, leaving someone who—yes—is pious, but doesn't seem to be much more than that.

Finally, Shabbat comes to a close, and everyone heads to bed. I wait impatiently for Salome to rock herself to sleep and for my parents' snores to drift down the hall. I want to talk to Miriam, really talk, find out what, if anything, is brewing beneath her skin.

I'm ashamed that I haven't done it before. I mean, we talk, but it's about who's going to brush Salome's teeth and if Mom will be up for the day's chores.

It's time to have a heart-to-heart with my daughter.

"Miriam," I whisper.

She gurgles a little. "Everything okay?"

"Everything isn't okay."

She sits up, staring at me. "You seem okay."

"I want to talk to you about how not okay things are."

Moonlight streams through the window, casting Miriam in a spotlight. Looking beatific, she tucks her knees underneath her chin. "Did you really run off to Brooklyn with a random guy?"

I rear back, surprised by her words, which have the snarky bite of a teenager. "How do you know that? Mom sent you and Salome out of the living room."

She points to a vent by her bed. "I can hear everything."

"I saw the assassination happen. For real."

"Why were you even there?"

I drop my voice to a whisper. "Because this whole idea is insane, and I wanted someone to validate exactly how insane it is."

"What's insane?"

"That you're going to give birth to the Mashiach ben David and save the Jewish people. Nothing in the history of the world and our religion supports that." My volume increases. "Most Jewish people would have a huge problem with it as would a fair number of Christians and Muslims. There's a reason why Dad and Dr. Elías barely mention it outside of here."

Miriam tosses her hair. "Of course, I believe it. I'm going to be famous, the mother of the man who saves the Jewish people."

I frown. "That's why you're doing this? To be famous?"

She sniffs. "It's about what being famous can get me."

"Which is what?"

She swipes an arm around the shabby bedroom. "Out of this dump, for starters."

"And . . ."

"Into someplace beautiful." She plucks at the sleeve of her nightgown. "And into some way prettier clothes. I don't mind dressing modestly, but I'm so tired of cheap, ugly skirts and blouses in black and gray." She tips her head toward the window. "Do you see that?"

I peer through the window, but nothing catches my eye. It's the same old, same old of the Lower East Side in the 21st century. Television screens flicker in the building across from us. Below, tipsy singles step out of a dive bar, their steps loopy and unsure.

"What am I supposed to be seeing?"

Miriam points to the apartment directly across from us. "Through that window."

I follow her gaze. On-screen, three women with long, carefully curled locks walk through an expensive boutique, fingering silk dresses and velvet scarves. Similar features mark them as sisters.

"I could wear that." Miriam's voice pulses with longing.

On the show, the thinnest and prettiest sister removes a top from the rack. It's a perfect shape for an observant Jewish girl with flared sleeves that hit below the elbow and a neckline that covers the collarbone.

"That's why you're going to go through with this?" I ask. "For pretty clothes?"

"It's about more than that." Miriam smiles radiantly. "I get everything, and I can give everything." Her dark eyes shine brighter than the moon. "I'm going to be the people's mother."

"Do you think Dr. Elías is full of it?" I ask, trying to catch her off guard. "That he has another reason for this wild goose chase around the country?"

Miriam doesn't answer for a while, her attention snagged by the sisters arguing over a full-length duster in midnight-blue felted wool.

"I love dark blue," she says. "Black is boring, and gray is the color of rain."

"Are you going to put your health, maybe even your life, at risk, so you can have a wardrobe of dark blue?"

On-screen, the plainest sister tries on a dark green dress with long sleeves and a jewel neck.

She nods. "Only a year or so until I can wear that when I present the Mashiach ben David to the world."

I bite my lip, not sure of what to say to Miriam. She doesn't believe it either, but she's conjured up a closet of beautiful clothes to get herself there.

I sweep my eyes around our bedroom in understanding. This life is the pits. Everything we own is old or ugly or stained—often all three. And even though plenty of people around the world would kill for our old furniture and cheap clothing, it doesn't change that Miriam feels our poverty strongly.

She wants soft, pretty, expensive things. She wants to be important, necessary even after her purpose has been fulfilled. She wants to be loved by people she doesn't know because the people who do love her want her to be someone no one should have to be. If I were her and had lived her life, I would do anything to get to the next part of my life, which would, at least, be better superficially.

I turn my attention back to the television program. The plain sister is twirling in the dress, and she looks beautiful, so beautiful.

"I watch every night through the window," Miriam says. "Wherever we've lived, I've always found a way to watch television. This show is my favorite. They go shopping in almost every episode. I also like awards shows. The dresses . . . even the ones I can't wear . . . they're so gorgeous." She sighs. "I love clothes. One day, I'd love to start my own line for Jewish women who want to look fashionable yet still be modest."

"You can barely hem a skirt."

She shrugs. "When I'm the mother of the Mashiach ben David, I can hire people to do that."

"There are other ways to get pretty dresses." Even to my ear, I sound sharp and parental. "In fact, most of those ways are a lot more honest and moral than what you're going to do."

Miriam's eyes stay glued to the television across the street as I wait and wait for her to answer.

"Maybe," she says finally. "But I don't lose anything beyond a few months of my life, which isn't much of a life anyway." She shrugs. "The way I see it? It can't hurt, and it might even help me and the Jewish people. Besides, do you know what I heard a couple of weeks ago?"

I shake my head.

"I wasn't doing anything special, just going to the thrift store with Mom to buy Salome a new pair of shoes. There were these two guys in front of us, acting like they were the only people around and talking about girls, who they called . . ." She frowns, not wanting to say the word.

"I know what you want to say."

Miriam continues. "Anyway, they were talking about the sister of a friend who's thirteen. One guy said, 'I would knock her up if she weren't thirteen. The other said, 'Old enough to bleed, old enough to breed." Her voice has a shrill, outraged tone. "I don't think they were religious, seeing as they were drinking beer out of cans in paper bags." She looks at me, her eyes wide with outrage. "Is it that crazy when normal people think the same thing?"

I flop onto the bed. Miriam isn't quite the paper doll I thought she was, but she's not stuffed with much more than cotton.

I sigh. She has no reason to put her foot down, so I have to stand up for her and get her out of this mess not of our making.

Which means she needs to trust me.

"Do you," I say, sitting up and adjusting my hair over my shoulder, "want to hear the story I didn't tell Mom and Dad?"

M iriam pretends not to hear me. On the television, the three sisters are at home, unpacking their new clothes to show their mother.

"It involves kissing." I pump up the word *kissing* to the point where I'm worried my parents might have heard me.

It does the trick.

With a lingering look at the television, Miriam rolls to face me. "Kissing?"

I nod. "The guy who killed Father O'Donnell is a for-real assassin. He works for this organization of billionaires who pay assassins to kill evil people."

Miriam rolls her eyes. "You're making that up."

I shake my head slowly. "Not even a little bit. They have hackers who do research, and then they send someone in to do the, um, deed. Normally, they make it look like a home invasion, but they wanted Father O'Donnell's to be public." I stop and then add, "So everyone would know about his transgressions."

"Even if that's true, why were you at the church in the middle of the night? I can't imagine you went in, thinking that you would just stroll up to the priest and start talking about our crazy family and how we've been chosen to save the Jewish people."

"I got there earlier . . ."

"And then . . ."

"And then I fell asleep." I cough in embarrassment. "Under one of the pews. I was tired because I hadn't been sleeping much. Anyway, no one was around, and I thought a quick nap would help me focus. When I woke up, it was happening. There was nothing I could do, nowhere I could go."

Miriam's eyes widen. "You saw him stab Father O'Donnell?"

"You can't imagine the amount of blood." I close my eyes, remembering. "How red it was," I whisper.

"Were you scared?"

"Terrified. Then it got worse." I pause for dramatic effect. "He saw me."

"And?" Her voice is high and breathless.

"He kidnapped me. He didn't have any choice. I was evidence."

Miriam's mouth flops open. "Where did he take you?"

"To his apartment in Queens."

"Where in Queens?"

I bite my lip. "I'm not sure. He bought us pizza from a mom-and-pop shop that stays open all night—that's the only clue I have." I hesitate as memories of Bowie crowd my brain. I'd been so terrified of him then, and all he'd wanted to do was buy me dinner.

I continue. "Anyway, it doesn't matter because he's left the country."

"To do another job?"

I nod as Miriam gasps.

"He's a professional assassin. What do you think he's going to do? Open a tea shop?" I snap. I roll onto my side and finger the knife I slipped under my pillow when Miriam was pulling on her nightgown. Wherever Bowie is, I hope he knows I'm keeping my promise.

"Do something other than murder people. Because that's awful." She gives me a pointed look. "Way worse than anything Dr. Elías is planning."

I correct her. "He murders bad people. People who molest dozens of children and get away with it. He stops them from doing it ever again."

Miriam narrows her eyes at me. "You saw him murder Father O'Donnell and were kidnapped by him for a week. Yet you're defending him. You have . . . what's it called?"

"Stockholm Syndrome. Which I, in fact, don't have."

"But you liked him!"

I sigh. "He was nice. He cooked for me. We talked about life." Saying it out loud to Miriam makes it feel like Bowie and I had nothing special, even though we did.

"What does this have to do with kissing?" Miriam smacks her forehead. "You kissed him. That's—wait—did you like it?"

"It's the nicest thing ever." I have no intention of telling Miriam about all the other things that are even nicer than the nicest thing ever.

"Is he Jewish?"

"I doubt it."

"That's off-limits," Miriam says. "You can't date anyone who isn't."

This is true—kind of. Jewishness is passed down through the mother regardless if the father is or isn't Jewish. Which means in my fantasy world, that if I had children with Bowie, then they would be Jewish and raised as such.

"He's a wonderful person," I say.

"I'm sure the assassin is *wonderful*," Miriam says. "Just, like, the best guy ever." She sniffs. "Even if I wasn't in this situation, I would only marry a Jewish man."

Good and evil exist in every race, religion, and gender."

"Maybe, but he's immoral in all of them, seeing as he's a murderer." Her tone has the haughtiness of someone who has never had her life script rewritten in a few seconds. "You should be ashamed. Mom and Dad would explode if they found out."

I cross my arms about to give Miriam a piece of my mind. I

open my mouth and then close it as I remember that I need her to trust me.

"Anyway, I want to talk to you about something," I say. "While I was gone, I realized something. I don't think we're practicing Judaism right."

"Of course we are. We eat kosher and dress modestly and follow all the other rules. Mom freaked out a couple of weeks ago when she thought I was using a pen before Shabbat was over. All Dad does is study and daven. I'm pure and modest." She preens. "I never forget what my purpose is as a Jewish girl."

"But that's only part of it. Jewish people don't live isolated from each other. They live in communities, have friends, go to weddings and bar mitzvahs at temples with actual rabbis. We don't do any of that. And, any time, it started to look like we were getting a little close to a community when we traveled, Dr. Elías whisked us away to a new city." I meet Miriam's eyes. "Remember West Palm Beach? We were talking about officially joining a synagogue to put down roots, and then Dr. Elías made us go to Minneapolis. In the dead of winter."

"So what? That's ancient history. We're in New York until we go to Israel." She glances out the window to the television but frowns when it's a commercial for pantyhose. "At least, there's plenty to see here."

"There's a reason for all of this, and it's not because Dr. Elías is worried about the survival of the Jewish people."

"And what would that reason be?"

"Dr. Elías is taking orders from someone higher up. Someone who runs a criminal enterprise."

"You sound crazy," Miriam says. She tries for a flippant tone, but her words shake.

I shrug helplessly, unable to tell her more. "That's why I want to get you out here. Once you give birth, we're useless, which is to say expendable."

Miriam cowers into her covers, looking pale and younger than her age. "Why are you telling me this?"

"Remember the organization I told you about? The one the assassin works for?"

She nods.

"They sent one of their guys to watch over us for a few days. All I have to do is find the guy in a dark blue hoodie and ask him what kind of pizza he likes. If he says sausage, then I know I can trust him. He'll take us someplace safe."

Miriam doesn't say anything, just flips on to her back and stares at the ceiling. "And where would that be?"

"I don't have exact details, but probably a new town with new identities. A place where we can lie low for a while."

She laughs without humor. "I'm surrounded by loony people with loony plans. I can either give birth to the Mashiach ben David, if the baby I give birth to actually has enough smarts to turn into, like, the best leader of all time, or I can put my trust in an organization of assassins to end up in the middle of nowhere, not even being myself anymore."

Miriam shifts her gaze to the television screen across the street. On it, credits roll as the three sisters sashay down the street, swinging their shopping bags. They throw their arms around each other and smile for the camera.

"Miriam," I say tentatively. "Listen to me. Let me help you."

She pulls the covers up to her chin. "Goodnight, Hannah."

29

On Saturday, an opportunity arrives in the early evening. The sun has slid well below the horizon, so Shabbat has officially ended. Mom takes Miriam and Salome to the market to help her carry groceries for tonight's dinner while I scrub a mountain load of dishes. In New York, it's easier to go shopping every day, buying just what we need, keeping the trek up and down the five flights of stairs to a daily minimum that Mom can manage.

Dad and Dr. Elías settle around the dining table to stare at some spreadsheets. They do this every week, adding donations and subtracting expenses to create a report that they . . .

I actually don't know what they do with the report. I'd assumed it was for the charity's records, but now, I suspect they send it to someone.

Jāzeps. Who probably uses it to keep tabs on us.

While Dr. Elías and Dad enter numbers and talk in low voices, I wash dishes in the kitchen. I'm biding my time, scrubbing the same pot over and over, my hands pruning in the hot, soapy water. Something in the air tells me that this might be the moment I need.

I need to get my hands on Dr. Elías's laptop and find out why he's spent the last dozen-plus years zigzagging the country with one family and nothing to show for it. He has no wife; he hasn't even been on a date to my knowledge. He has no beautiful home, no eye-catching convertible, and no fancy watches. He doesn't have any new professional contacts or speaking engagements or even a book deal for all the research he's done.

He's in the same place he was except for the worn-out soles on his shoes and a head of hair that's gradually lightened from black to silver.

There's a good reason for that, and I bet that reason is on his laptop.

I bend my head and scrub the pot for the fifth time, ignoring how raw my skin feels.

Finally, Dr. Elías slams the laptop shut and pushes it away. Dad stands and reaches for two glasses and a bottle of Manischewitz wine.

I remember Angelina's words. "You will never be ready. The perfect moment will never arrive. Opportunities are made, not presented."

So I make my opportunity. I toss a dozen cookies on a plate, grab the least chipped dishes we have, and two cloth napkins. I tweak my lips upward into a smile and march toward them.

I plunk down my bounty on the table. "You two look like you could use a snack."

They turn to me, their eyebrows lifting in surprise.

I shrug casually. "We have leftovers. Also, I want you to know how happy I am to be home." I grin extra hard until my cheeks ache from the pressure.

They smile back, their eyes blank with gullibility.

I pretend to spy the laptop. "There's not enough space." I swoop the computer into my chest with one arm while, with the other, I spread out the plates and napkins. "I'll put it in the kitchen until you're done."

Dr. Elías's eyes taper at the corners, but he waves his hand in approval.

"Make sure that not a drop of water penetrates it," he says. "I have documents of consequence stored on that."

For a second, I stop, hearing his voice for the first time, rather than listening to his words. It's tinny, almost whiny, and I can't figure out why I listened to him for so long.

"Of course," I say. "I'll be right there to watch over it." I strive for a bright tone. "Just a few more dishes to dry."

"You're a good girl, Hannah," Dad says. For the first time in a long time, he sounds as if he loves and values me.

Just a couple of weeks ago, this would have knocked me in the knees, sent me reeling with joy. Now, after Bowie, who told me within the first couple of hours that I was smart and a good talker, it's too little, too late, from someone who I'm beginning to realize is a big dupe.

But these are thoughts for another time. So I keep my smile firm and shuffle my feet and say thanks before I stroll—as slowly as I can make myself—back to the kitchen.

Once there, I quickly wipe the sink clean. I place a different dishtowel in the sink and then put the laptop on it. From the dining table, Dad and Dr. Elías can see me, but they won't be able to see what I'm doing.

I flip the top open to get down to business.

It's so easy that I almost stop, sure that Dr. Elías has set up some trap on his laptop.

He hasn't.

Because he feels so safe that he doesn't need to use anything other than minimal protection.

Everything Angelina taught me is useless. Dr. Elías's password takes exactly one attempt to guess.

Because the password is *password*.

It only gets easier from there. He has a well-organized desktop with all his files lined up like soldiers. It takes me ten seconds of scanning to find the folder labeled *Photos*.

I start to double click the folder and then remember that I'm not alone, that I'm not supposed to be seeing this. I fake dry a dish as I check out Dr. Elías and Dad.

They suspect nothing as they chew through the cookies and sip their wine.

Baruch HaShem, I whisper to myself, feeling if there's ever a time to thank G-d, then this would be it.

I forget to do that again because I open the folder named *Photos* and find what I'm looking for—*Favorites*. I almost throw up as I scroll through the contents.

Dr. Elías is all kinds of messed up. He likes young girls. Not almost-legal high school seniors, but Lolita-like nymphs aged twelve and thirteen. I scroll through picture after picture as vomit rises in my throat. Most of the girls appear Asian or Eastern European, their unlined skin contrasting with their dead eyes and slumped shoulders.

How could anyone think this is okay? I think. *It is awful, the absolute worst type of exploitation where a man elevates his desire above a girl's actual life.*

This is why it's been no big deal for Dr. Elías to spin us like straw with the promise of gold at the end. When you're this terrible, acts of evil probably don't seem like a big deal.

The squawk of the buzzer sends adrenaline flooding through me. Quickly, I shove the flash drive into the jack and start moving stuff onto it.

Mom speaks through the static of the buzzer, asking Dad to go downstairs and help her.

"C'mon, c'mon," I whisper under my breath. There's no time to get it all. My hope is to get enough so that it will be enough.

I yank the flash drive out and shove it into my sweater pocket. I start to cheer, but my hooray gets stuck in my throat because footsteps are approaching.

Although I'm close, so close, I can't get Dr. Elías' laptop out of the sink, close the lid, and stow it somewhere innocuous before he turns the corner, sees me with my hands in the sink, clutching his laptop, the lip open.

"I believe I told you to stow that in a locale where it wouldn't be dampened," Dr. Elías says.

30

I force a toothy grin at Dr. Elías. "It got a few specks of food on it. I was washing it off and wanted to check the inside to make sure nothing got there. Just in case." I say it too fast, the words tumbling out one after the other. The tempo rather than my tone gives away my guilt.

He rips it from my hands. "I see nothing."

"I must have done a good job."

"But of course, Hannah. You did a stellar job."

The front door slams. Dad has left, which means I'm here with a sicko for seven minutes since that's the amount of time it will take Dad to trudge downstairs and then upstairs with my family and the groceries.

Dr. Elías appears to have had the same thought. He flings an arm around me and claps another against my mouth. He pushes me against the sink, so I can't go anywhere. He's no Bowie, but still, I struggle against him.

"Why were you looking through my laptop?"

"I wasn't. I promise."

"Banish the good girl act. I know where you have been, and I know what you have seen."

My spine stiffens. "Which is where? Seeing what precisely?"

If I weren't so terrified, I would laugh. I'm imitating Angelina.

"You witnessed the assassination of Father O'Donnell and then absconded with the assassin."

"Allow me to correct you, darling. I didn't abscond with the assassin. The assassin kidnapped me. Held against my will until, for reasons unbeknownst to me, I was allowed to go."

Being Angelina is fun. Somehow, a British accent makes me sound smart and important.

Dr. Elías isn't having any of it. Tightening his grip on me, he quickly releases one hand and feels around in one of my pockets. It's the wrong one, but that just makes it worse because he'll check the next one and find the flash drive there.

"I knew you would be trouble when you returned. It takes only a few hours away from your faith and family to soil a pious woman into a mouthy trollop." He glares at me.

"Actually, you were the one to soil me by making have a baby when I was fourteen."

I struggle against him, wiggling this way and that, as he uses his body to push me harder against the sink. He dips his hand into the next pocket and paws around until his fingers close around the flash drive.

"Nice effort, darling," he says tauntingly as he lifts the flash drive high in the air.

I slump against the sink, all my bravado at channeling Angelina evaporated.

That's when I remember that I can be someone other than Angelina or myself. I can be Bowie.

Plan B, I say to myself as I prime my ears to figure out where my family is. I hear nothing, which means Dad is still walking down the stairs. I have at least six minutes because it always takes longer to go up than to go down. Not because the stairs are steep, although they are, but because four people, one of them only four-years-old, laden with bags is a long and unpleasant ordeal.

It's go time. I'm going to get as much information from Dr. Elías before my family returns.

I squeeze a few tears out of my eyes as I slowly shift my right hand around my back. He has me in a vise grip, which means I can't escape, but I can get ready.

"Are you going to kill me?" I ask, my voice thin and high.

Internally, I slow clap at my performance. Two weeks ago, I couldn't have pretended to like broccoli under the threat of death. Now, I'm lying like a pro.

"Of course not." Dr. Elías laughs. "But I do know someone who will be delighted to do the honors."

I pitch my wails higher as I move my hand further around my back, feeling around for the knife in its sheath. "Jāzeps?" I sigh silently with relief when I grip it. "He's a criminal, one of the worst, right?"

"How do you know about Jāzeps?" Dr. Elías inches closer to me as I place a hand on top of the one that's holding the knife.

I peek at the clock on the kitchen stove. Five minutes until my family returns. I take a deep breath as I tap my knife. I have to keep my wits about me.

"The assassin guy told me Jāzeps has been following us for years."

He exhales. "You know too much, Hannah. You could have enjoyed a lovely life in a few years, living in Israel and married to a man who'd treat the mother of Miriam like a queen. Instead," his tone sharpens, "you decided to get inquisitive."

"Why are you doing this? What's in it for you?" I ask, listening for the sound of steps on the stairs. It's faint, but it's there. Salome is crying and refusing to walk up the stairs, which means Dad has to carry her. That adds thirty seconds, maybe even a minute.

"To save the Jewish people from another Holocaust. I know the signs, and anti-Semitism is sweeping the world once again. This time, though, we can be ready." His tone has the cold, colorless sound of lines that have been recited one too many times.

"You could fight anti-Semitism without doing any of this."

He snorts. "Because that's never been tried before—fighting anti-Semitism." He glares at me. "If you had performed the research that I have, then you would understand that reasonable measures have little utility. To stop anti-Semitism, the act must be prodigious, one that forces the hand of the world. No one should care if the miracle is made in a Petri dish. The miracles back then could likely be explained by or enacted using science. It did not make them any less miraculous or any less desirous."

"Why this way?" I ask. "I was fourteen when I gave birth to Miriam, and she won't be much older when she gives birth to Mashiach ben David." With my hand tight against the knife, I lean toward Dr. Elías. "Times have changed. No one thinks fourteen-year-olds having babies is a good thing, no matter how perfect their lineage is. Why do you think anyone is going to do anything except say *yuck*?"

Dr. Elías leans forward until our noses are almost touching. I start to recoil, but he grabs my chin to force me to stay meeting his eyes.

"You, your gender, is the problem. Even with all the advances in technology and medicine, people remain as immoral as ever. And I have thought and thought about it, and the only logical conclusion is that giving women rights is detrimental to virtue."

My jaw drops as I shift my eyes to the clock. Three minutes.

"Working outside the home, having sex before marriage, accessing birth control?" He shakes his head. "It's eroding the moral fabric of society. No decent man seeks a woman . . ." He sneers at me. "Such as yourself." He drops his hand from my chin.

He thinks I'm going to be upset by his insult, but I'm anything but. "And your solution is what?"

"For us to return to how things were for men and women."

"Which is what? Marrying girls off at twelve and thirteen before they know anything about the world? Because that's what you want? To have a twelve-year-old openly?" I should've resisted, but I can't. Anyway, it's not like Dr. Elías doesn't know what I found on his laptop.

He stares at me for a long moment. "Do you know why I became religious?"

I shake my head.

"Because it made me feel like less of a freak of nature. It was normal—even expected—for men to desire girls who'd just become women, to want to build lives with these newly formed women, to sculpt them in the way that only an older, sophisticated man can."

I check him out for signs of lying, but his eyes are bulging with honesty.

"But the world changes," I say. "Just because something was normal then, doesn't mean it should be normal now." I tip my head down to point at my blouse and skirt. "Nobody wears tunics and veils anymore, not even the Haredi. Nobody lives in tents and herds goats. Nobody lives to be hundreds and hundreds of years old. So why . . ." I struggle to control my anger at Dr. Elías's justification for his behavior. "Should your perversion be normalized?"

31

I've gone too far. As soon as the words leave my mouth, I regret it. Dr. Elías' expression darkens.

"I can't turn it off and make as if it is not encoded into my DNA." Then, he starts to bellyache. "It is all there, written into the beginning of our time. People try to disassemble or explain it away, but those are flawed responses. It is normal. I am normal. It is normal, even to HaShem. Why else would girls still ripen to womanhood at twelve and thirteen?"

My vision turns red at his disrespect. I lift the knife out of the sheath a few inches. It feels like it's on fire as all my anger channels itself into it.

I force myself to tune my ears to the sounds of footsteps outside the front door. I'd become so involved in my conversation with Dr. Elías that I'd forgotten to listen for my family returning.

Salome is shrieking as Dad tries to calm her. Mom is panting as Miriam takes steps with even plods. They're two staircases away, which is to say I have around ninety seconds. Maybe a few more if Salome is being more difficult than usual.

"How does Jāzeps fit into this?"

"You shouldn't know about him, Hannah."

"Tell me," I say in a silky voice, "what does Jāzeps do for you?

Because I've been listening to you talk for a while now, and you sound like you have no idea what you're talking about. So I'm guessing Jāzeps has something big on you."

"I thought you'd already figured it out, you little snoop."

I choose my words carefully. "It doesn't seem like pictures and videos would be enough."

"You're smarter than you need to be, Hannah. Every couple of months, I receive a reward."

"A reward?"

"Don't be obtuse. You know what I mean." Dr. Elías pouts. "It's not the life I would have chosen, but my needs get met and I'm well-suited to the work."

The footsteps are getting louder. They're on the final staircase. I have less than a minute. But I have one more question that I have to ask if I can get it past the bile in my throat.

"Do my parents know about your . . . rewards and stuff?" I pull the last inch of the knife from its sheath. I have less than a minute left.

He laughs without humor. "They've never come out and said it, but they think I'm gay and that I have chosen this life to help keep myself on the straight-and-narrow." He shrugs. "If I step off every once in a while, then there's no need for a fuss because I always get back on." He pulls himself up to his full height. "Plus, I have worked miracles, slowly but surely, taking individuals who nominally practice Judaism and leading them through the scorched annals of history to understand the blessings of HaShem that await. I have reunited fathers and sons, turning them as one to the coming of the Mashiach ben David."

My body is vibrating. Now I understand why Mom and Dad felt safe having Dr. Elías with us—a family with young girls. They assumed his liking was for something else, not realizing how dangerous he was. Black dots race in front of my eyes, but I blink them away. I can't faint now. Salome's wails are getting louder. My family is a handful of steps away.

"Alcoholics stop drinking. Addicts quit doing drugs." I hold the knife flat against my leg. "You could have gotten help and learned to stop."

Dr. Elías's lips droop before he looks up, victorious. "Fortunately, Hannah, no one cares what you think." He begins to walk, pulling me with him, to drag me somewhere awful, to do something awful to me.

I don't give him the chance.

I wriggle out of his grip and drop my knees. Quicker than the beat of my heart, I chop one of his Achilles' tendons in half. I don't do a very good job. My cut is uneven and shaky, but I slice through it mainly because the blade is sharp and my adrenaline is pumping. Then, I do the next one as Dr. Elías gasps in pain and surprise. I do an even worse job on this one, but it doesn't matter.

He collapses to the floor, moaning and clutching the backs of his ankles. The flash drive falls out of his pocket and bounces across the floor to my feet. I pick it up and step over Dr. Elías's body.

"I hope it hurts," I say. Bowie said he didn't want to make his victims suffer, but I want Dr. Elías to suffer at least a little. I'd like to think Bowie would agree.

I sheathe my knife and smooth my skirt. Salome's yowls are so loud that it sounds as if she's already in the apartment. It's only a matter of seconds before they're here. In my head, I rehearse my lines as I walk toward the front door.

I meet everyone in the hallway. Salome is having a full-blown temper tantrum with tears streaming down her cheeks and snot dribbling out of her nose. Miriam is kneeling beside her, trying to convince Salome to come inside. The only positive is that her shrill wails cover Dr. Elías's more guttural ones.

Mom and Dad are sagging with exhaustion, their arms burdened with shopping bags from kosher butchers, bakeries, and greengrocers.

"Chicken was on sale," Mom says. "I bought more than planned."

Miriam sports her normal beatific expression save her eyes,

which flick upward. It's not quite an eye roll, but it's close enough of one that I can guess her thoughts. *This life is the pits. Instead of shopping for pretty clothes, I'm stuck watching my mother argue with the baker over the price of a dozen bagels.*

Everyone is spent, ready for a quiet dinner and an early bedtime.

Except that's not what's going to happen. What's going to happen is they're going to find Dr. Elías in the kitchen, his Achilles' tendons gashed and bloody.

I need to be long gone before that with Miriam in tow.

"I broke a glass in the kitchen," I announce. "But the handheld vacuum cleaner is dead, so I'm stepping out for batteries."

Mom nods as she edges through the door to put down the groceries. She collapses in a chair as Dad soothes Salome.

I lean into Miriam. "Come with me. I just looked out the window and saw one of the sisters from that show you like. The pretty one is at the fancy gelato place on the corner."

Miriam crosses her arms. "Really?"

I didn't miss a beat. "Really. She's wearing a purple dress with a high neck and a maxi skirt. You have to see it."

"I don't know," she says although her eyes light up.

"Five minutes." I jut my chin to our parents. "Miriam forgot the bag with the challah in it downstairs. We're going to get it."

No one even looks up, which is good because the bag in question is resting beside the front door, the challah sticking out of the top like a middle finger.

"Come on," I hiss.

She nods, and we race down the stairs and out the door into the dark twilight of a chilly fall evening. I blink for a moment, letting my eyes adjust to the light.

I scan the crowd, trying to pinpoint a guy in a navy blue hoodie. It feels like an hour passes, but in reality, it's more like seconds until I find him, wearing tan dress pants that seem at odds with the informality of his hoodie. He leans against a brick wall, staring at his phone.

I tug Miriam's hand. "This way."

I run to the hoodie man who looks up, his head jerking back at our presence in front of him. I lash my arms around Miriam to prevent her from escaping.

"What kind of pizza do you like?" My voice thrums with urgency.

He doesn't say anything for a minute, just stares at me stupidly until his lips curve into a smile. "How about sausage," he says, pronouncing *about* like *aboot*.

Something in his voice makes me hesitate, but I'm too agitated to think it through. "Yes," I say.

A flurry of motion catches my attention. A gigantic man—tall and muscular—is running to us. He is also wearing a hoodie, but it's more gray than blue. Something about how lightly he moves makes me think of Bowie, but he can't be Bowie because Bowie is on the other side of the world.

Just a guy out for an evening jog, I think. *Even still, the way he's running at us is scaring me.*

"We need to get out of here," I say in a low scream. "Fast."

Miriam strains against me, but I tighten my arms around her. Hoodie man leads us to a sedan parked a few feet away.

I throw Miriam into the car and leap in behind her, slamming the door shut. Hoodie man jumps in and thrusts his key in the ignition.

"Buckle up, ladies," he says. "Might be a bit of a rough ride, eh." Then, he rolls up one of those bulletproof dividers found in cabs and police cars.

The clack of the lock echoes around the car.

My heart slams against my chest as everything clicks into place.

32

I have just willingly gotten into the car of one of Jāzeps's henchmen. I rattle the door handle, but nothing happens. Frantically, I search for a way to get out of the car, but there's zilch. I collapse onto the hard leather seat.

Minutes pass as we drive from the Lower East Side to the Holland Tunnel, our destination somewhere outside of New York City.

I stare out the window, my hands clasped over my knife.

At least I still have that.

Touching the knife reminds me of Bowie and the last time I was riding off to an unknown fate. I somehow doubt this will turn out like that did, the blood-thirsty assassin revealed to a man who dances, makes frittatas, kills for moral reasons, and steals my heart.

I place my head in my hands. The possibility is strong that Jāzeps will kill me, a girl whose usefulness has been exhausted for some time now. Miriam is the one he's interested in, which is why I have to figure out how to convince him to leave us alone.

Speaking of Miriam, I drop my hands and shift my eyes to her. She's curled in the seat, her gaze averted.

My jaw drops as I figure out why we ended up here. "You told!" I exclaim. "How could you? I trusted you."

"I had to."

"You had to what? Get me killed?"

"Don't be silly. No one is going to kill you." She goes for a glib tone, but it comes out like the mewling of a scared kitten.

"Of course, he's going to kill me. I've been working with the good guys." I scowl at her. "Which I was doing to help you."

Miriam looks down.

"Who did you tell?" I ask in a strangled scream. "Dr. Elías?"

"He said I did the right thing."

"Why?" I ask. "Why would you do that? I'm your mother." Even with the seriousness of the situation, I rear back. Although Miriam and I both know this, I've never said it out loud.

She keeps her eyes fixed on her skirt, her lips tightening. "Because this is my ticket out of here."

I widen my eyes at her. "And where, exactly, will this ticket take you? You're going to be the mother of the supposed Mashiach ben David. You might not have to work as hard, but you'd definitely have to be good all the time plus try to make sure your son is better than good all the time."

"I have an idea," she says in a small voice.

"Let me guess. It involves starring in your own reality show —*Bring up the Mashiach ben David*."

She doesn't respond for a minute as my fingers touch my parted lips. Miriam really is that young and naive.

Finally, she whispers, "It doesn't have to be a reality show. But I do want pretty clothes and to be well known."

I clap my hand to my forehead. "You're an idiot, Miriam. The guy funding this is a career criminal. He operates chat rooms and websites filled with foul child pornography. Then, he blackmails the users, so he gets paid on the front and back end." My volume increases. "Does that sound like the type of person who's going to care about your reality-show hopes and dreams?"

Miriam bristles. "I have rights too. He just can't impregnate me."

I glare at her. "He can and he will. And nobody will care until it's too late because nobody cares about us. We have no friends, no extended family, no synagogue, no schools to ask about us when we disappear."

My volume increases. "We're pawns in a sick man's game, and you blew our opportunity to get away," I yell. "You might even cost me my life."

"I hate Mom and Dad," she bursts out. "I hate them so much. I would do anything to get away from them and this stupid life where I'm nothing but free labor."

I sigh and look out the window: nothing to see but a highway stretching in front of us. A sign to my right says we're entering Pennsylvania.

I peek over at Miriam, whose lips are twisted in fear and self-righteous anger. My rage evaporates in pity for her. She is so young and isolated with no friends her age and nothing to do beyond help with childcare and housework. This might have been normal for most of human history, but in the 21st century, it makes for a life of endless white space. This is probably the first time she felt like she could assert herself.

I pat her leg. "It's hard for you to imagine, but we were in a terrible place for such a long time. Dr. Elías showed Mom and Dad a way forward—a crazy way—but not any crazier than plenty of other things that happened in the Tanakh. Plus, you wouldn't be here otherwise."

"What are we going to do?" The tendons stand out on her neck.

"I'll think of something." My voice rings with conviction, which is the opposite of how I feel.

I sink into my seat. I need a plan, a rock-solid one that will get us out of this mess. I frantically think of something—anything—I can use to convince Jāzeps not to execute something that shouldn't be executed by any man.

I'm also hoping I can figure out how to convince him not to kill me.

But I've got nothing because I'm a woman with no practical experience about to face off with a legendary career criminal.

33

The man in tan drives us for a while through Pennsylvania, until the commuter towns thin out and it's just small villages, some rich, some poor, but all surprisingly remote and sleepy for being so close to New York and Philadelphia.

The sun is slipping below a ridge of trees as we turn onto a back road. We pull up to a checkpoint, which is guarded by two men in tan slacks and dress shirts. Apparently, Jāzeps has an entire tan-clothed army at his beck and call.

Miriam and I haven't spoken since she asked me what the plan is, which I still don't have beyond trying to convince Jāzeps that his plan isn't just crazy. It isn't going to work. Sure, he can impregnate Miriam and force a barely teenager to have a baby, but as for the rest? How is he going to get all the Jewish people back to Israel, build the Third Temple—a site that's conveniently occupied by a mosque—and usher in a thousand years of peace and prosperity?

There has to be more to the plan, and I'm going to do my best to find out what it is. If nothing else, at least I'll know why we've been living like this for over a dozen years.

Maybe understanding that will be enough to comfort me when Jāzeps kills me.

I shelve my dark thoughts because a different man in tan swings the car door open and gestures for us to exit.

"I'm sorry," Miriam whispers as she gets out. Her eyes are red, as if she's been crying.

My heart clenches. She's my child whose interaction with the world has been through televisions glimpsed through windows. I have to protect her.

I unbuckle my seat belt, the strap zipping across the knife I still have on me.

I freeze. What if we have to go through a metal detector? The knife will set it off, and the four inches of protection I have will be taken away. I take a deep breath and yowl.

A man in tan jerks his hand at me, indicating that I should exit. Instead, I rock myself back and forth as I pretend to cry hysterically.

"I'm not getting out. I refuse to walk myself to my death."

The man in town shuffles his feet. Finally, cursing under his breath, he grabs me and slides my rigid body across the seat until I'm staggering against him.

"Sorry about that," he says, his pronunciation marking him as another Canadian.

Are they all Canadian? I think as I continue to scream and fight against him.

He drags me to the door of what is not a house, not even a mansion, but a compound with tan-dressed men milling outside, guns dangling from their waists. Although it looks nice enough with ornate shrubbery and an imposing front door with a brass knocker, the tall walls and small windows suggest its real purpose —to protect someone inside.

I continue to tussle with the man in tan as he hauls me up the stairs and into the foyer.

Lights blare. Sirens shriek.

"I don't want to die," I scream. This man in tan tosses me over his shoulder as he stomps through the metal detector. I pelt his back with my fists and yank at his thinning hair. Inside, I feel almost giddy. I did it. I got into Jāzeps's home with my knife.

I don't know where Bowie is, but in my head, I tell him thank you: for the knife, for the lesson in using that knife, and for all the ways he, by just being him, helped me. I will almost surely lose any fight, but at least I can go down trying.

"I've got a gun," the man in tan says as he shoves me off of him. "That's why the metal detector went off."

Off-balance, I tumble into one of those small but fancy chairs rich people like. I shift uncomfortably in the velvet seat as I scope out the room.

At first glance, it looks like a picture I once saw of Versailles with all the satiny settees and spindly end tables clustered together. Then, my eyes zoom in. Whatever Jāzeps is spending his money on, it's not on the upkeep of his home. Dust blankets the tables, and stains streak the settees. Mud speckles what was once probably an expensive rug but is now a chewed-up rag thanks to the army of men trampling across it.

I count each man in tan. Nine of them to one of me. My blood chills. It should be nine of them to two of us because Miriam is supposed to be here.

I frantically gaze around the room, my heartbeat increasing in tempo every inch I scan that doesn't contain Miriam.

My desire to keep my knife has caused me to lose track of her. I slump in the chair, my fake tears giving way to real ones. She's gone, and I have few to no ways of getting her back.

The odds are overwhelming. I'm going to die, and Miriam is going to be sacrificed to fulfill some stupid perversion of the prophecy. I hug myself, suddenly so cold. I force myself to think of happy thoughts. If I have to die, then I'll go into the dark with a heart lighted with happy memories.

There are the memories of my family, of course, but it's the week I spent with Bowie and Angelina that's at the forefront of my mind. Although I was—I remember Bowie's phrase—an unexpected and unconventional guest, it was the happiest I'd been in a long time. Because I got to be me. Because I got to be me with people who got me. Who I got in return.

"Hannah."

Surprised out of my grief for a life that had barely gotten started, I look up. Another man in tan is looming over me.

He jerks his head toward a long hall. "This way."

Robotically, I stand and follow him. Although my body leads me forward, my thoughts take me backward, into Bowie's arms.

To happier times.

The man in tan deposits me in front of a large door.

He nods toward it. "He's expecting you."

He must be Jāzeps. I force myself to be calm and push the door. It doesn't open. I try again, this time with more force. Nothing. Finally, I slam my weight against the door, and it swings open as I tumble into a gloomy room.

I blink as my eyes adjust to the dimness. It's a study with bookshelves stretching from floor to ceiling. They overflow with stacks of leather-bound books, the titles etched in gold. I squint to decipher the squiggly print, but give up. It's in Hebrew, a language I only recognize a few words of.

I turn my head. A gigantic desk looms in front of a roaring fire. Behind it sits Jāzeps. He is grinning.

"Do you recognize me, Hannah, mother of Miriam?"

I nod. "You came after I gave birth."

His dark eyes twinkle in the firelight. He still looks like a Jewish Santa Claus with a long, crinkly white beard and round, red cheeks like apples. He's attired all in black, a kippah firmly settled on his head.

Nothing about his appearance would single him out from any other observant Jew with his black coat and payot, the sidelocks of men who believe that G-d forbids shaving the corners of one's head.

Yet something seems off. I scan him up and down, trying to figure out what it is. Then, my eyes snag on his fingernails, which are of different lengths. The fourth finger sprouts a long nail as does the pinky. The others are chewed to the quick.

I furrow my brow. *That's odd.* Judaism has rules for every part of life, including nail care. Jewish people cut their fingernails out of order, starting with the ring finger of the left hand to end with the pinky of the right hand. Clearly, this is a rule Jāzeps doesn't care to follow.

Jāzeps sweeps his arm to a straight-backed chair, which lifts me from my thoughts.

"Sit," he says, his voice high and cheery.

I perch gingerly in it as my heart slaps against my chest. I don't know what's about to happen, but I doubt it's going to be good. Jāzeps stares at me, his eyes shiny and bright, his lips curved joyously.

I touch my hair. Jāzeps's warmth contrasts with everything I know about his criminal activities. The silence stretches between us as I get more and more flustered, wringing my hands and pulling at my blouse. He continues to grin serenely at me.

"Why are all your henchmen Canadian?" I ask, trying to stall.

He laughs, one sweet and melodic, like a ditty played on a piano.

"What an astute question, mother of Miriam." He leans forward. "They are Canadian because I am Canadian."

"Okay," I say unsurely.

"I need loyalty—absolute loyalty—so I must exploit whatever bonds I can. A country, though, is not enough to ensure a man's fidelity to a cause he is unlikely to believe in." He continues to beam. "So I find men who are in the throes of despair. I offer them money, the opportunity to wield a big weapon, women and liquor as bonuses." If possible, his eyes twinkle even more. "It works—has worked—for decades." He shrugs. "They aren't the best, but they are cheap and grateful, which means I can have an army of them to do whatever I ask."

In spite of the fire, I shiver. "So safety in numbers?"

"Exactly," he says in a pleased tone.

"Why did you leave Canada?" I squirm. I'm not sure why I'm asking him questions beyond buying myself time.

"It is the country that made me who I am, but it is also the country that would not allow me to become who I could be."

"And who is that?"

He issued another tinkling laugh. "That, mother of Miriam, will take some time, time that we—"

"I want to know," I burst in. "I deserve to know, seeing as I'm part of it."

His smile remains in place although his eyes darken. "Perhaps you do. So you can understand." He reaches for a walkie talkie and presses a few buttons. He keeps his voice low, but I gather he's ordering dinner and telling whoever's on the other end to make sure Miriam is comfortable.

As he talks, I inhale and exhale, forcing myself to be calm, which I absolutely must be. Because I have a plan, a frail, desperate one. I'm going to learn everything I can about Jāzeps and exploit whatever chink in his armor I can find.

And, if that doesn't work, then I'm going to put my knife to work.

A knock on the door startles me. I look up, sure my face is giving my plan away, as a heavy-set woman walks in. Her hair is covered with a mitpachat, a headscarf. Her dark skirt brushes her ankles, and a shapeless vest hangs over her blouse. She must be Haredi, a form of Judaism that's even more devout than the Modern Orthodoxy my family practices. Over the tray she's carrying, she sniffs at my knee-length skirt and blouse. Neither is baggy enough to hide my female figure.

Jāzeps gestures for me to follow him to a small table by a window. As I sit, the woman begins unloading the tray: chamin, challah, potato kugel, and brisket with dried apricots. She gives me one last up and down look before leaving, clearly judging my lack of modesty. That and I'm an unmarried woman about to have dinner with a man I'm not related to.

Little does she know how immodest I am with my plan to attack the man in front of me with the knife stuffed into the waistband of my skirt, which is hidden by my sweater.

Jāzeps pours me a small glass of Manischewitz wine and points to the dishes cluttering the table. "Eat," he says. "I'll be offended if you don't. I spend little on the finer things in life, but I have found that a belly full of good food helps maintain my focus."

I spoon some chamin on my plate. This is my second dinner in less than two weeks that's with a criminal, yet they couldn't be more different. With Bowie, I thought I was going to die. With Jāzeps, I know I'm going to die. With Bowie, I thought he was a hardened criminal. With Jāzeps, I know he is a hardened criminal.

I don't know if it's going to be my last meal or not, but I'm going to make the most of it.

"Where in Canada were you born?" I ask.

"Toronto. A few years after World War II."

I have a mouthful of chamin, so I tilt my head to indicate interest.

"My parents were Jewish refugees from Latvia." He chews a bite of brisket thoughtfully. "Their experience was different from the stories you hear about the Holocaust in Germany and Poland. It was, as all the stories are of the Jewish people, filled with terror and degradation."

I scan my brain for what I know about the experience of Latvian Jews and come up with a big fat zero.

"My father lived in Riga, my mother in the outer vicinity. After the Nazis arrived in 1941, they were moved to the Riga Ghetto, along with 23,000 other Jews. A barbed-wire fence kept them from coming and going save for work when the Latvian police kept a close and brutal watch. Food was scarce and only given to those who labored. My father, barely sixteen at the time, worked to feed his pregnant mother and younger siblings."

Jāzeps smiles at me as I shiver. His cheerful demeanor is deeply unsettling, considering what I know about him.

"One day, when he left as part of a work column, he saw my mother. For him, it was love at first sight, which was rather lucky for her. Even with the small amount of food my father received, he managed to save a few crusts for her. In moments snatched between marching in and out of the Ghetto, he would pass them to her."

I stir my spoon around the chamin, tense and already anticipating the bend in the story from love to horror.

"It was a mean, penurious life, but they had their romance to add beauty and excitement to their days." He strokes his wine glass with a long pinky nail. "But then it got much worse."

"What happened?"

"Their families were killed in the Rumbula Massacre in 1941. Along with over 20,000 other Jews.

"What's the Rumbula Massacre?"

He chuckles. "The history of anti-Semitism is so long and wide-ranging that you," he points at me, "an observant Jewish girl, doesn't know about the Rumbula Massacre."

"Sorry," I mutter. "I would like to know."

He simpers at me. "You have nothing to be sorry for, mother of Miriam. Most people, many Jewish people included, have never heard of the Rumbula Massacre."

"Okay," I say, fiddling with my skirt, feeling guilty about my ignorance.

"Himmler instructed his men to clear the Riga Ghetto to make room for German and Austrian Jews. To do it quickly and efficiently, the men dug inverted pyramids to form murder pits. The plan was to literally march the prisoners to their own graves. Germans did the shootings, not Latvians, to demonstrate their superior marksmanship."

My hands shake.

"I'd say they succeeded," he says.

"How did your parents escape the Massacre?"

"They were hiding in a tiny, almost invisible garret, when the Security Police came calling. In columns of one thousand, the Jews were marched to Rumbula, stripped of their clothes and valuables, forced on top of those who'd already been shot, and then shot themselves."

I gasp.

"My parents were exploring the passion one experiences in the throes of a first and only love."

My cheeks go hot as my thoughts go immediately to Bowie and our one night of passion. To cover my discomfort, I take a big swig of wine and then wish I hadn't. The wine has gone sour. Jāzeps has all the money in the world, and he doesn't seem to spend it on anything beyond Jewish comfort food and an army of tan-dressed men.

He's spending it on something, I think. *No one profits that deeply from criminality not to spend it on something.*

Jāzeps's expression doesn't change, but his voice dips a notch lower. "They, of course, figured out what was happening and waited it out, trembling in each other's arms, knowing the world would be upside down when they rejoined it." His tone is lackadaisical, as if he's reciting the daily specials at a restaurant.

A tear trickles down my cheek.

"Yes, it is horrible, mother of Miriam, but cheer up. I'm here, so obviously, they survived."

I press my lips together, but I can't smile. Not in the middle of this nightmare of a story.

"They survived, for years! Then the Nazis liquidated the Ghetto and sent them to a concentration camp that fortunately did not specialize in death. When the Red Army advanced, my parents were evacuated to Poland, where they made it until the war ended."

I have stopped eating, my fork dangling from my fingers, my chamin growing cold on my plate. I'd forgotten where I was, why I was here, as I listened to Jāzeps excavate the history of my people I didn't even know. I could use a minute to gather myself for the next chapter in the story of how someone as twisted and evil as Jāzeps came to be.

He doesn't give me a second. Instead, he continues. "Even with all the horrors, Canada gave them the promise of hope. A new country, a new marriage, a chance to practice their religion in peace." His smile slips as he shakes his head sorrowfully. "But the trauma had burrowed deep inside of them."

He stops to stare at me. The twinkle in his eyes sparks into fire. "Children can forget, build new and happier memories to cover the old and ugly ones. Adults can philosophize the hurt away, then pass down lessons to a new generation. But young adults?" he asks. "They neither have the youth nor the maturity to do those things. Instead, the trauma stays fresh and potent." He smiles. "Do you remember what it's like to be a young adult?"

I *don't remember what it's like to be a young adult,* I scream in my head. *Because I never got to be one. You took all those experiences from me.*

Instead, I mumble something that sounds like yes but means no.

"They tried their best to make a life worth living in Toronto. But once I came, the hope—which should have increased—diminished. They were scared that a peaceful country like Canada would eventually turn on them."

I close my eyes. Canada, America, you name it. For Jewish people, a current of fear flows under all the liberty-and-justice-for-all slogans. In the minute it takes to recite the Pledge of Allegiance, anti-Semitism could spring up and take hold of the nation's imagination.

"Their thoughts were based in reality. Although they lived in the Jewish neighborhood, right off Bathurst Street, any time they ventured beyond the familiar enclave, they felt hatred, both real and imagined. If an old lady sniffed at my mother's hat, my mother would assume she was sniffing because my mother was Jewish." Jāzeps shrugs. "Maybe she or maybe she wasn't, but it didn't matter. My mother took it all as an insult. She rarely left a dozen-block radius."

"And your father?" I ask.

"He reacted differently. He became an alcoholic to face his demons. He was an accountant, and he made a point to go after the big Gentile accounts. He would sell himself as a penny-pinching Jew before coming home to swallow Canadian whiskey."

"In celebration of landing the accounts?"

He shook his head. "To deal with his complex emotions. His Jewishness had once made him hunted. Now he was the hunter, exploiting the very thing that had almost gotten him killed."

Although Jāzeps stays smiling, the skin around his eyelids droops. "Alcohol and anxiety don't mix well. They manifest themselves in screaming and long periods of angry silence until the only bond that remained between them was a shared past. Even that was tested daily."

"It sounds . . ." I trail off, not sure if I should say how terrible I think it was. Even with all my family's problems, my parents had stayed strong.

"Unpleasant," he finishes for me. "It was a dysfunctional household where I was left to fend for myself. By the time I was five, I could make myself dinner and put myself down to sleep before getting myself up to go to school."

"I don't know what to say," I manage to get out. My family is dysfunctional, but we eat our meals together and wish each other goodnight before we bedtime, after which we get up as a unit in the morning.

He waves a hand. "It was a different world then."

I lean forward. Jāzeps might be a criminal, but he is a gifted storyteller. "How did you do that?"

The twinkle in his eyes flares. "I learned many things living off Bathurst Street."

"What kinds of things?"

Jāzeps stares off into the distance, as if remembering. Then, he swings his gaze at me. All the chuckles and grins have been extinguished, and his face is hard and cunning. I shiver and look down. I hadn't forgotten that Jāzeps is a criminal, but his demeanor had softened my vigilance. Then, as if I had imagined it, his eyes are twinkling, the smile pasted back in place.

I sit up straight and park my fork by the plate. "What kinds of things?" I repeat.

"That even I—a tiny Jewish boy no smarter than the average child—could become powerful. People who would have bullied me for my small stature and skinny frame did no such thing. Instead, they respected me, begged for my opinions on matters, recommended me to their friends. I discovered power, and the best power is the one you hold over people who hate you."

"What did the Gentiles do to you?"

He trills a little *he he*. "You don't need me to elaborate about the acts of anti-Semitism that regularly occur, do you, mother of Miriam?"

"I . . ." I'm not quite sure how to answer the question. Because, yes, I know what he's talking about.

He nods wisely. "Ignorance and small-mindedness accrue. Sliced enough times, paper cuts become gushing wounds."

Silence falls between us. I try to think of something to say before I remember the question I asked that set us on this tangent.

"How did you do it?" I ask again. "Become someone important even though you looked like you were anything but."

His eyes sparkle. "How do you think I did it, mother of Miriam?"

I frown, thinking back through what Bowie and Angelina told me.

"You found out people's secrets. And then you bribed them, so they would pay you to keep your mouth shut," I say.

He doubles over in hysterics as I look away.

"You are smart, mother of Miriam. Smarter than you should be." He pauses before picking up again. "In the beginning, the secrets weren't that exciting." Jāzeps sniffs. "Who was having an affair with his secretary. Who charged a quarter to let high school boys feel her breasts. Who gambled the vacation money away. Who beat their children too hard."

I nod.

"So many people, so many secrets." He points at himself. "And me, just the tiniest, happiest boy who happened to be in the right place at the right time." He issues another chuckle. "Which I made into the best place at the best time once I learned how easy it was."

So the happiness is an act, verified by Jāzeps himself.

"But were they scared of? An upset wife? A few whispers? A dirty look? A withdrawal of an invitation to Shabbat at the Cohens? I kept their secrets and manipulated their secrets, but I knew that if I kept at it, then I was never going to be more than a small-time hustler." He pauses. "Lesson number one: Think bigger."

He smiles with all his teeth bared. "I needed to find better secrets, the kind that people will pay anything to keep."

"Pedophilia." I state it rather than ask it.

"Correct. A crime so foul that it is unforgivable." He giggles. "People will do anything to keep that perversion from coming to light."

"How did you figure that out?"

"I've always been small, so I could easily sneak into places and hide. One day, I hid in the bushes in front of the piano teacher's house. She wasn't a very good teacher, but the neighborhood felt sorry for her. Her husband had died some years earlier, and she had four plain teenage daughters who would take a while to catch husbands." He shakes his head. "So the neighborhood sent their children to her."

I nod, guessing where this is going.

"Her first pupil was a little boy of perhaps eight or nine. Upon his arrival, she plied him with cookies and a glass of milk. Then, he sat down to play. For every wrong note, she made him remove his clothes." He tilts his head at me. "Can you guess what happened next?"

"Yes," I say, almost unable to get the word through my revulsion.

"But knowing what she was doing wasn't enough. I needed evidence." His eyes brighten, and he titters. "Every child learns soon enough that his or her word against an adult is useless."

"Pictures?" I ask.

He grins at me. "Yes. Pictures. So I took the money I'd saved and bought myself a top-of-the-line Polaroid camera. Of course, it was nothing like the cameras on the cheapest cell phones these days, but it was enough. I spent a week hiding in the bushes and snapping pictures before confronting her." He holds up a finger. "That's when I learned lesson number two."

"Which was?"

"Targets must have value."

"She didn't have money?"

"That, but more importantly, she had no reason to stay and pay."

I bite my lip.

"To make the type of money I wanted, I had to target two types of individuals: those who were incentivized to make a large, one-time payment or those who could cobble together small, regular payments. The piano teacher could do neither. She made a couple of payments before picking up and moving in the middle of the night." He shrugs. "She wasn't worth the effort to track down."

Vomit swirls in the back of my throat. Although the piano teacher is probably long dead by now, she must have continued her disgusting lessons with little boys.

My stomach is roiling at our conversation. Jāzeps may be the worst person I've ever met, and that's saying something since I spent years living next to Dr. Elías. Jāzeps exploits evil, magnifies it, normalizes it, and then profits from it.

The question pulses: *But for what end result? He has to know his plan is too crazy to succeed.*

Behind my back, I touch my knife. I'm going to find out, and after I do, I'm putting a stop to it, regardless of what I might lose.

Which is to say my life.

Internally, I carefully place my thoughts to the side and turn my attention back to Jāzeps, who has put on an expression of mock sadness. The skin around his eyes is bunched up, his lips stretched tight.

In a quiet voice, he continues his story. "The internet gave me everything I wanted. I could gather all the pederasts into one place and let them reveal themselves. Then, like a vulture, I can swoop down and collect evidence of their sins."

"Why not turn them over to the police and keep them from hurting more children?" I yell, so sick from Jāzeps's revelations I don't care anymore if it gets me in trouble. "You had evidence. You could have put them away forever and made the world a better place."

He fixes me with his eyes that are lacquered hard and impenetrable. "I am making the world a better place. You will see that soon enough." He pauses. "Besides, do you think locking up a few pederasts solves the problem? I can assure it does not because there's always more to take their place."

"But you never tried any other way." My volume increases until I'm shrieking. "All the children you could have helped, all the lives you could have made better. And you didn't. Not even one."

Jāzeps stares at me for a long while. Then, abruptly, he reaches out and grabs my wrist as I recoil. "I am making the world a better place, mother of Miriam." He throws me an ugly smile. "Do you think I'm telling you this for fun?"

"No," I manage to get out.

"I'm telling you, so you understand."

"Understand what?" I ask.

"That you must die to save the Jewish people." He shakes his head. "I cannot let you do anything to disrupt the delicate balance of the plan."

"I've followed your family for a long time," Jāzeps says, interrupting my fearful thoughts.

"How long?" I rub my hands against my arms, trying to stop my shaking. I would give anything to walk away from all of this and never look back.

But I can't. Because he has Miriam, and I'm not leaving here without her unless . . .

I push the thought of my imminent death from my mind. I need to focus and find something I can exploit.

"Since before you were born."

"How is that even possible?"

He chuckles. "Very easily."

I tilt my head, willing him to say more.

"Many years ago, I became bored with making money. The things I could spend it on were so banal: jewels, a fast car, a vacation at a sunny resort in the middle of winter. So I turned my hand to charity, donating to Jewish organizations that did everything from fight hunger to arrange trips to Israel."

He shrugs. "But I discovered a problem."

"What problem?"

"Donating money earned from my work is difficult. Small amounts here and there can go unnoticed, but large sums arouse interest. Since charities are not taxed, their accounting must be pristine. Sooner or later, I would be unmasked, and that created quite a quandary. I had a fortune, and nothing of impact to spend it on."

"Impact?" I ask.

"I made all this money with the intention of using it to alter the fortunes of the Jewish people dramatically, and I'd failed. I decided to turn my attention to a topic that had been niggling at me since my ill-fated venture to donate money. Why would societies accept help to feed its people from a Jewish charity but not accept the Jewish people who donated that money? I began researching my ancestors, which is to say I studied the history of Judaism. Quickly, I became consumed by it, traveling from library to library, from internet site to internet site, to continue my family tree and to piece together their stories. I kept going further and further back in time until I'd created a massive forest of branches."

He gazes at me. "That's how I found your family. We are related. Did you know that?"

I shake my head as, internally, my throat burns.

"Your family caught my attention due to your genetics." He smiles at me as if I should be happy about this. "Your family's lineage was a gift, but it was one I didn't quite know how to use."

Because I'm a person, I scream in my head, *not a branch on a tree for you to cut off and use as a weapon for yourself.*

I wish I could say this to Jāzeps, but I can't. Not yet, at least.

"But the world changed, thanks to technology, which pointed my way forward." He smiles at me. "My career has severely limited my social life. The internet changed that. On one of the genealogy forums I frequented, I met NewJew. We became fast friends, discussing anti-Semitism, genealogy, and the fate of the Jewish people. NewJew had a background in academia, so he could tease out nuances in texts that evaded me. Together, we concocted a plan that would use modern technology to bring about an ancient prophecy. NewJew, a former Catholic, was quite adamant about whom we should use to bring about the Mashiach ben David. He was also quite attached to the idea that the births needed to be from a virgin."

He smiles. "The Jewish people put no stock in the idea that the Mashiach ben David should be born of a virgin, but NewJew wore me down with his arguments. Plus, as he pointed out again and again, for the first time in the history of humanity, we have the technology to architect a virgin birth. No longer did a woman have to have intercourse to become pregnant. No longer did she have to deliver vaginally, thus breaking the hymen. Although the Jewish kings and warriors are long gone, their DNA survives, and we could use it to create the Mashiach ben David. For the longest time, NewJew and I talked about this in the abstract, a fun intellectual exercise. But then it became real to me."

"How?" I ask.

"Something happened that had happened a thousand times before. I was traveling to Israel, where my permanent home is, and had a layover in Germany."

He points at himself. "I did something stupid. I fell asleep in the airport. Although it was the middle of the afternoon and the airport was bustling, I awoke to find that I had been pickpocketed. Instead of a wallet bulging with cash, I awoke to find a note in the handwriting of a first grader that said, *You deserve it you dirty Jew*." He shakes his head. "It wasn't the loss of the money. It was that I had been targeted because I was a Jewish person. In *Germany*, the country of the Holocaust, that takes measures to ensure another one won't happen. My response was guilt. I held myself responsible."

Jāzeps stares into the distance before looking back at me, his smile tacked into place. "I'd been presented with much evidence to suggest anti-Semitism was thriving, yet I, by doing nothing, was doing something to contribute to its spread. My guilt grew and grew until it consumed me. I had money and resources. If I didn't do something, then who would? That's when I decided to make the plan a reality. I told NewJew of my decision."

"I'm assuming NewJew was Dr. Elías?"

He beams at me. "Correct, mother of Miriam. You should know that Dr. Elías is no doctor, though. He never defended his dissertation."

"Oh," I say, surprisingly unsurprised. In retrospect, it makes sense. Dr. Elías had always glossed over where his doctorate was from.

"A little college in New Mexico," Dr. Elías would say with a wave of his hand. "You won't have heard of it although the professors were excellent."

When the questions got more specific, he dodged them.

"I don't even remember what I studied, to be honest," he'd say as he fiddled with his papers. "It was long ago, and my interests have since moved on."

Now, I get why he spoke so convincingly. He had a lot of practice in telling the same lies over and over.

"Why didn't he defend his dissertation?"

"He was kicked out. His doctoral advisor had invited Dr. Elías to his home to have dinner and go through some last notes. A couple of hours later, he found Dr. Elías outside, peeking through the window of his twelve-year-old daughter's bedroom."

Jāzeps shakes his head. "He could have been a brilliant academic. For all his flaws, he possesses considerable intellectual gifts."

"What flaws?" I ask even though I have plenty of evidence to suggest what, exactly, those flaws are.

"He likes very young girls. He considered the priesthood for a while as that would allow him unquestioning access to them, but then he discovered he was Jewish. So he went into education. He was a principal at a small elementary school in a poor district. Parents were absent or barely present thanks to addiction or incarceration or working three jobs to pay the rent."

My brain speeds ahead. "He had easy access to the kids because their parents weren't around."

Jāzeps nods. "Kids who were hungry for everything: food, new shoes, a few words of affection. It took so little to groom them. A piece of candy and a pat on the back, and they were his."

"How did you find this out about him?"

"Dr. Elías felt safe, the king of a tiny fiefdom that allowed him to indulge his fantasies." Jāzeps smiles at me. "That's when he made his mistake."

"Mistake," I echo.

He nods. "He wanted to share his good fortune with others who had a similar perversion."

"That's disgusting," I say as the dinner I swallowed several hours earlier makes a beeline up my throat.

"I don't disagree. But, to Dr. Elías, he thought he was doing something positive." His lips turn down. "I know it is hard for you to understand, but even criminals have morals. We draw lines that we refuse to cross. I, for instance, will not create any content for pederasts. I only share and recycle that content."

"And profit from it when you could have turned them over to the police." I couldn't resist adding for the second time.

"Crime is very profitable. And in the end, when I have made the world peaceful and prosperous for the Jewish people, you will understand that the ends justify the means."

I didn't meet Jāzeps's eyes, sure my hatred for him will shine through. Instead, I keep him talking, my hands out of sight as I mentally go through all the training from Bowie. "How did Dr. Elías go from being a run-of-the-mill pervert to being your number-one henchman?"

"When a man is desperate, he makes grave, irreversible decisions." He fixes his eyes on me, all the humor suddenly gone. "In the beginning, Dr. Elías promised all the usual things when I came for him. He promised to stop for good. He promised to dedicate his life to HaShem. He promised to give me everything he had, which wasn't worth much of anything."

"You didn't believe him?"

He shook his head. "Of course not. I'm sure he, like all the rest, meant it when he made these promises. But men like him never stop, that I know for a fact, having been in the business for half a century. They hibernate until they think they're safe. Then, like the snakes that they are, they strike again."

"That's awful," I say to myself.

"It is, and Dr. Elías would have ended up just like the rest except for one thing."

"NewJew had emailed me, saying he had made some mistakes in his life and would be moving far away where he could start anew. He signed off wishing me luck with the plan."

"He was going to run?"

"It was his only solution until I showed him another way forward." Jāzeps gazes at me with bright eyes. "I had to show him another way forward."

I frown. "Why?"

"Because he knew the plan. If he wasn't going to be part of it, then he could easily thwart it or, worse, clue someone in who might try to stop it."

In my head, I say, *I'm going to stop the plan.* Out loud, I say, "How did you find out that Dr. Elías was the same person you had been talking to online?"

"Immediately after receiving his message, I put my hackers to the task." He laughs as I shiver. Now that I'm getting to know him, his laughter has a sinister ring that shows inside, he's as dark and hard as a lump of coal.

"It didn't take them long to piece together that Dr. Elías was both my friend and target." His eyes twinkle. "Now that was a conundrum. But my success can be attributed to my ability to unite problems into solutions. And, at this time, I had another problem."

"We were the problem," I say. "You needed to set your plan in motion."

He smiles in a pleased way. "You are correct. I needed someone to manage your family. I thought quite hard about it and concluded that Dr. Elías would be a good candidate. I flew to meet him, and once he got over his shock, he agreed. He was the one who came up with our cover of traveling the country to raise money for the cause."

"Is there actually any money? Is it going to be used for anything?"

38

Jāzeps nods. "There is money, and it has all been legitimately raised and accounted for. When the time comes, it will be used to bring the Jewish people back to Israel and build the Third Temple."

Above his smile, Jāzeps's eyes are two sharp points. "Your family, though, wasn't meandering through the country just to raise money. You were there to verify Jewish identity and gather information. I know, for sure, who is Jewish and who is not. I know the tactics to take when we call them back to Israel. Dr. Elías and your father did wonderful work."

Jāzeps beams at me, like I should be pleased. Instead, I'm anything but, which spurs me to ask the question that I've wanted to ask since we left for Mexico.

"Why did you make me have Miriam at fourteen?" I ask. "Why do you want Miriam to have the Mashiach ben David at fourteen? Is it really because that's how old girls were thousands of years ago?"

His lips tweak downward. "I'm sorry about the timing. I would have preferred to wait a few years, but . . ." He points at himself. "I am not young, and this plan is a long-ranging one. HaShem has kept me in good health, but that could change in a moment." He holds my gaze, his eyes twinkling. "And I must stay alive until the plan has accrued enough momentum to fulfill itself."

I stitch my mouth into a tight line.

I was fourteen, I yell in my head. *Fourteen. And maybe you being old was a reason, but I doubt it was the main one. You did it because I was too young to say no, to fight back, to understand how wrong it was. It's why you're not going to wait with Miriam either.*

"Miriam will be thankful for the experience. She has been chosen, after all. As you were." Although he stays smiling, his tone is bored, condescending, a cat who's done toying with the mouse and ready to go for the kill.

"Shouldn't HaShem craft the coming of the Mashiach ben David?" I ask in a desperate voice. I'm going to have to act soon, and unlike the anger I had toward Dr. Elías, which fueled me, I feel tired and sad. Which might be exactly the state Jāzeps wants me in. That way, I'll go off to my fate quietly.

He snorts impatiently. "HaShem is a provider, giving me everything I need to erect the Messianic age, including a family with perfect lineage, unlimited funds, and the technology to do so." His face brightens. "With HaShem, all things are possible, but only if one is willing to do the work of assembly."

Work, I think to myself. *Making fourteen-year-old girls have babies isn't work. It's sick.*

My eyes sweep over the heavy, dusty books, my brain working overtime. Then, it clicks, why everything turned bad when it did.

"Did you mastermind all the terrible things that happened to us the year I turned eleven?"

He adopts a grave expression. "I'm afraid I did. Your parents needed to be one step away from total ruin for them to agree to such an outlandish plan. So—and I'm very sorry about this—I devised the modern version of the plagues. Instead of frogs and boils, I gave your family unemployment and a house fire. Your mother's Graves' disease was written into her genes. Enough stress, and it would turn on."

I sit up straight, my backbone rigid as the knife that lays against it, fire singing the edges of my soul. All the fatigue I felt earlier has fled, and I'm angry, angrier than I've ever been in my life: at my parents, at Dr. Elías, at Jāzeps, but most of all myself. For years, we traipsed around the country, visiting Jewish community after Jewish community, and I'd never questioned why we were doing what we were doing until it was too late. Now, I'm going to die, and my daughter is going to be sacrificed to fulfill a criminal's insane plan.

"The prophecies are clear. The Mashiach ben David must bring the Jewish people to Israel. As soon as Miriam is impregnated, I will set that part of the plan in action." His eyes sparkle. "And come they will. The prophecy is written into Maimonides' 13 Principles of Faith. Not to believe it is to not be Jewish. Even when they were at the gates of the gas chambers, the Jewish people sang 'Ani Ma'amin'—I believe in the coming of Mashiach!"

"There's no way you can get all the Jewish people back to Israel."

"I don't need them all to come at once. I need a few to come in the beginning. Whether they come to marvel, to argue, to mock, or to pray, it doesn't matter, just that they come. From there, I'll work in waves, calling the Haredi and the Orthodox first and then the less observant."

"Some still aren't going to come."

Jāzeps shrugs. "That is their problem, which they will ultimately have to take up with HaShem." He grins to himself. "As for me, I may have spent the better part of my life profiting from filth, but I will make up for it for by returning as many Jewish people as possible to Israel, thus preventing another genocide. Once gathered, we will regroup and regain our power to usher in an era of tranquility." He swings his eyes to me. "Don't you want that, mother of Miriam? For our people to be safe, to be happy, to live in peace for all their years?"

I stand up, my arms rigid at my side. "I don't want my daughter to have a baby at fourteen. That's what I want. As for the coming of the Mashiach ben David, that's up to HaShem. It doesn't have anything to do with you, and it most definitely should not have anything to do with Miriam and me." I say it in one breath, too scared to stop.

He removes his walkie talkie and whispers a few words into it to call, I assume, a man in tan or a few dozen of them. Then, he rises, his eyes never leaving mine. Although he's shorter than me, I cower.

All the fake happiness has fallen away, and in its place are flinty eyes and an iron backbone. "I am the Mashiach ben Joseph," Jāzeps hisses. "I am the suffering one, and oh, have I suffered, wading in all that is perverse so that I could accrue enough money to wage war against the forces that oppress Israel. I will die for the prophecy, but," Jāzeps extends his index finger toward me, "not today. That is for you. Your death will be just another one of the many calamities before the Mashiach ben David comes to redeem us."

The black dots come for me, flocking across my eyes like buzzards as I get it, the final link uniting all the pieces into a whole. Jāzeps has cast himself as a prophet from a little-known vision of the four craftsmen in Zechariah, and it doesn't matter whether it's true or not true because it's true to him.

"I waited and waited," he says, his tone icy. "Because the Mashiach ben Joseph is not necessary to bring the Mashiach ben David. The Jewish people only needed to return to Israel to meet those who've already returned, so we, as a people, could practice one Shabbat perfectly, practice two Shabbats perfectly, or just repent for a single day. Any one of these would bring the Mashiach ben David. Yet everyone did nothing, too wrapped up in their little lives that have little to do with HaShem."

He laughs, a mean, low one. "Every year on Passover, people raise their glasses and toast: 'Next year in Jerusalem,' yet no one books a ticket. The next year and all the years after, they say the same empty words."

I step away. Jāzeps is terrifying in his single-mindedness.

"After years of rigorous davening and intense frustration,

HaShem spoke to me. He told me I must anoint myself the Mashiach ben Joseph to force the issue. The Jewish people needed someone to spur them into action since they themselves would not do it."

Jāzeps smiles at me, but his eyes remain shrewd and hard. "And I'm close, so close. We, as a people, are close. Almost six thousand years of excruciating trials and tribulations are finally ending, and our rewards lay within reach."

He stretches a hand. "Come to me, mother of Miriam. We will drink to celebrate the future of the Jewish people."

I refuse his invitation. Like an actor who's been waiting for her cue, I drop to my knees and whip out my knife. I whack one of his Achilles' tendons, yet nothing happens. The blade won't *cut*. I push my entire weight against it, and, still, nothing happens.

My blood thrums in my ears as, too slowly, I understand why. Jāzeps is wearing thick leather boots, and I'm not strong enough and the blade isn't sharp enough to push through. My poor hacking of Dr. Eliás' Achilles tendons must have dulled the edge.

Above me, he laughs and laughs, a raspy one that sets my nerves to rattling. I try again, spurred by pure, raw adrenaline. Again—nothing, nothing, and more nothing.

I sit back on my heels as the pounding of a pair of boots down the hall clues me in to what's going to happen next. The door will fling open, a man in tan or an army of them will surround me, and I will die.

I shake my head. It can't be about me anymore, my silly, useless life that never got started. It can only be about Miriam.

I won't be able to save my life, but I just might be able to kill the plan. If Jāzeps isn't around to spur it forward with his money, then maybe it will die if he is dead.

Which is to say I have to kill Jāzeps.

39

Panting with effort and fear, I stand, yanking the knife back over my shoulder, just like Bowie did before he killed Father O'Donnell.

I thrust it forward, gasping in shock when it connects with Jāzeps' flesh-and-bone cavity. Although I'd given it my all, my aim was poor and I've struck his rib rather than the space between his ribs.

My stomach knots as I remember telling Bowie that I didn't want to learn to kill anyone, never dreaming I'd need to know how to do exactly that.

Jāzeps continues to laugh as I wiggle the knife upward before yanking it out. Blood trickles out of the tiny hole I've stabbed in him, but it's not enough. I know that, and he knows that.

The string of ha-has wraps around me like a noose, tightening my throat, cutting me off from oxygen and reason.

I step back, trying to put some distance between us.

My arms fold around my stomach as I truly *understand* myself. I can't kill Jāzeps. I won't kill Jāzeps. I let my weak knees start to bend as the boots sound louder outside the door.

I tried, I say to myself. *Hopefully, Miriam will know that I tried.*

Then, I jerk myself up. I am not giving in without more of a fight. Miriam has to know that I tried. If I give up now, here with Jāzaps, then she'll never know.

You don't have to kill him, I say to myself. *Wound him somewhere that doesn't take a lot of force. Then wound the next one the same way. And the one after that until you can get to Miriam.*

Jāzeps is still laughing. "You can't do it," he says. "I'm a defenseless old man, and you can't kill me because you want the plan to succeed. You know it's the only way."

He keeps talking, but I stop listening. Instead, I scan his body for places of weakness. Bowie told me to stay away from the trunk of the body, so I look for other places as Jāzeps' eyes bore into me, which gives me an idea. I adjust the blade in my hand as, mentally, I trace the line I want to slice.

The knob turns, throwing me forward into action. I take the knife and drag it across Jāzeps' forehead. I scrape through his skin but keep it from going into his skull. The result is exactly what I want. Blood pours into his eyes, blinding him. He screams as he tries to rub the blood out.

For a second I stare at him, red and crazed.

"Miriam is leaving with me," I say in a flat tone. "Figure out another way that doesn't involve impregnating my daughter."

The door swing opens with a bang. I lift my blade while making myself small. I turn to whatever man in tan has come to kill me.

"Hey, Snow White."

My clenched hand opens, and the knife clatters to the floor.

Bowie leaps into the room. The blade he's clutching glitters in the firelight. "You're doing great."

"I am?" It's the only thing I can think of to say. I stare at Bowie, my heart about to pop out of my chest. I thought I was never going to see him again, and here he is. I can't decide whether to cry or to kiss him.

"I needed time, and you gave that to me."

I gesture to the knife on the floor. "I couldn't kill him."

Jazeps starts to run, but the blood is still pouring into his eyes. He trips into Bowie, who wraps an arm around him.

Jāzeps's bloodied eyes bulge. "Give an old man mercy. Kill me. Now."

Bowie shakes his head. "No can do." He offers the knife to Jāzeps. "But you're welcome to do the honors." Bowie puts his arms up like a boxer, preventing Jāzeps from running.

Jāzeps takes the knife and lifts it high in the air. With a strength that belies his age, he shoves it deep inside his chest.

I want to look away, but I can't. Jāzeps collapses, and as he does, I see him for what he is.

For what he was.

Because the blood streaming out of him and the grayish tint of his skin means only one thing. He's dead, this deluded old man who'd fallen so far into darkness that the only way he thought he could go up again was by manipulating desperate people.

I turn to Bowie, who's holding his arms out. I run into them as, outside, sirens blare.

"It has to be a first," I say, relaxing into Bowie. He dips his head and kisses me as I try to remember what I was saying.

We're back at the apartment by the United Nations. Jāzeps and Dr. Elías have been taken into custody, and Miriam reunited with my parents. When we found her, cowering in a dust-covered bedroom, a plate of cold chamin beside her, she was shaken but unhurt and, most importantly, relieved to be done with the whole thing.

"I'm sorry," she said, throwing herself into my arms. "I want out."

As for me, after giving my statement to the police and making sure my family was reasonably informed about exactly how crazy Jāzeps was, I left.

"Later," I said to my parents, who were talking over each other, trying to figure out where I was going, who I was going to. I walked out the door and into Bowie's arms where we didn't talk at all for a solid twenty-four hours. Instead, we communed with our bodies as he made me stardust again and again.

Now, spent, we were lolling in bed, catching up.

"What has to be a first?" Bowie asks.

"The history of Judaism is filled with people pretending to be the Mashiach ben David."

"Christianity isn't much different. I read an article recently that said five people around the world claim to be the second incarnation of Jesus." Bowie shakes his head. "They all have bunches of followers too."

"But this is the first time anyone has pretended to be the Mashiach ben Joseph."

"There's another Mashiach?"

I nod. "The prophecy of the four craftsmen in Zechariah says that the Mashiach ben Joseph anticipates the Mashiach ben David. He wages war against the forces that oppress Israel and acts as the viceroy to the Mashiach ben David. Some scholars and rabbis even believe he will be the one to bring all the Jewish people to Israel."

"I never knew that."

"His passion for bringing the Jewish people back to Israel may have been real, but turning Miriam and me into circus freaks was a foul way to go about it." I sigh. "He lived for so long in the dark that his idea of fighting the dark was with more dark."

Bowie's phone buzzes, which he hands to me "Angelina," he says.

"Hello," I say shyly.

She greets me with a round of applause. "Bravo. You managed to do what no one else has done—get close to Jāzeps and then stay alive."

"It's not a big deal."

Angelina laughs. "Save the false modesty for another day, darling. You were fabulous."

"Did you know that Dr. Elīas' password was *password*?" I ask. "I was so excited to try everything you taught me, but I didn't end up using any of it."

"I'm not surprised. From what you told me, he seemed like a massive prat—all steam and no substance."

I smile, a big, goofy one, exhilarated by Angelina's praise. She was a tough nut to crack, but when I did, the result was sweet. "Thank you. For everything."

"The pleasure was all mine." She affects an arch tone. "I imagine you lovebirds have some cooing to do at each other, so I'll leave you to it."

"Come over for dinner soon?" I ask.

"Will you be serving something from that apartment's horrid pantry? It took days for me to get the taste of the coffee out of my mouth."

"We'll order in."

"Then count me in."

I hand the phone back to Bowie as he kisses me. "Angelina was right. You did great. You were with Jāzeps for hours, and not only did you stay alive, but you also got a ton of information from him."

"I couldn't kill him." I gulp, remembering the moment when I thought all was truly lost. "I wanted to."

"You kept him engaged long enough for my colleagues and me to fight our way in. His men weren't very competent, but there were a lot of them, so we needed the time. You gave us that."

"Where did you go after I went back to my family?"

Bowie grins. "I didn't go far. I was shadowing you up until you got into Jāzep's henchman's car."

"You were?"

He nods. "I told the Pact I wasn't going anywhere until I knew you were safe."

"Why weren't you around when I left with Miriam?"

"Because that would have been risky. Another guy was waiting for you, and he was supposed to take you to me. When he phoned to let me know you'd gotten into a car, I came as quickly as I could." His voice turns low. "But it was too late. The car was already pulling away."

"I saw you," I lay my head on his shoulder. "But I thought my mind was playing tricks on me."

Bowie rubs his cheek against mine. "I was worried," he says.

"More worried than I've been in years. But I should have known that you would be fine."

"How did you know where I was going?"

"The knife I gave you had a tracking device."

My eyebrows raise. "It did?"

His sky-blue eyes meet mine. "I'm sorry I didn't tell you. The more you knew, the more you could tell."

I flush, remembering how I'd told Miriam about the getaway option.

"Don't feel guilty about telling Miriam. It's what led us to Jāzeps."

"Jāzeps is dead, but what about Dr. Elías?"

Bowie laughs without humor. "Nothing pleasant. The law will take its course, and then the prison population will do its thing to Dr. Elías. They hate pedophiles."

I shiver before remembering that I'll never have anything to do with Dr. Elías again.

Bowie seems to read my mind. "What's next for you?"

I dip my head, so my hair falls in front of my face. "I'm not sure except for one thing."

"Which is?"

"I'm moving out."

"Have you told them?"

"Not yet, but I will," I say. "They'll have to face the truth now that Jāzeps and Dr. Elías aren't pulling their strings. I hope they go back to a normal life like we had in San Francisco."

"What about Miriam?"

"She would love nothing more than to have friends and wear pretty clothes."

"Are you okay leaving her?"

I sigh. "I'm conflicted. It's not because I don't love her. I do, but I've never been her mother even if I did give birth to her." I tug on a lock of hair. "I need to live for myself for a while."

"It's not official, but the Pact is arranging for the money your dad and Dr. Elías raised to come back to you." Bowie catches my expression. "Don't get excited. It's barely anything."

My eyes widen. "But we raised so much."

"Dr. Elías was skimming." Bowie pauses. "Scooping would be a better word. He planned to abandon ship as soon as it was time to go to Israel."

"What was he going to do?"

"He . . ." Bowie pauses. "Do you really want to know?"

"Start, and I'll tell you when to stop."

"He had bought in a place in Asia where the laws are laxer and—"

I hold a hand to stop him from saying more.

"Anyway, the money is enough to set your family up in a decent neighborhood close to a synagogue, here or in Israel. Your mom can get the treatment she needs for her Graves' disease."

I smile, overjoyed that my family is going to be able to get their life back on track. "It might take a while, but they'll be happy."

"How about you, Hannah? What would make you happy?" His eyes refuse to leave mine.

"To go to college. To move somewhere warm. To . . ." I trail off, not wanting to say what I really want to say, which is that I want to do these things with Bowie. It feels like everything happened for a reason so that I would end up here with him.

"Do you want company?" He shifts himself until the two new slices on his stomach are visible, the result of him killing two men in tan to rescue me. "Because I'm done with being an assassin. For good. I'm rejoining society as a law-abiding citizen."

"I . . ." I want to say, *Yes, I want company—your company*.

But I can't because I don't even know Bowie's real name.

He faces me and takes my hands in his, gazing at me, silently, until I'm melting.

"My real name is Justin Abbott. I'm thirty-two years old. I'm from a small town in Kentucky that you couldn't find on a map even if you tried. Everything I've told you about myself is true, and the truest thing is this. I'm in love with you, Hannah spelled the same way going forward as backward, and I want us to figure out what's next together. I'll do anything I can to make you happy for as long as you'll have me. My word is my bond."

He pauses as I wait, my heart thumping. "One more thing before you say anything. Your faith is a big part of who you are, so I did a deep dive into Judaism, and I could use it in my life, not having been in a house of worship, save for professional reasons . . ."

He stops as we both remember how it all started.

"Anyway, some of the temples will let me attend with you and learn more about what it means to be Jewish." Bowie doesn't blink as he holds my gaze. "Would that be okay? For us to go together, figure it out together?"

The tears come, and I can't stop them even if I wanted to. "May I still call you Bowie?"

He kisses me as an answer.

THE END

END NOTES

- Although *B is for Bowie* was born in the wild thicket of my imagination, I loosely hung my story on the prophecy of the Four Craftsmen: https://en.wikipedia. org/wiki/Four_Horns_and_Four_Craftsmen. You can read about the role of the Mashiach ben Joseph here: https://www.chabad.org/library/article_cdo/aid/ 101747/jewish/Appendix-II.htm . I was interested in how prophecy could intersect with science.
- Visit this website — https://www.davidicdynasty.org/ — to find out more about the descendants of King David.
- The inspiration for the novel is from this National Geographic article: https://www.nationalgeographic. com/magazine/2017/08/new-messiahs-jesus-christ-second-coming-photos/. Although it highlights the individuals who believe they are the second coming of Jesus Christ, it sparked my curiosity. Did the history of Judaism also contains individuals who believe they're the messiah? Spoiler alert: it does. More information here: https://en.wikipedia.org/ wiki/List_of_messiah_claimants
- More information about the Rumbula Massacre can be

accessed here: https://encyclopedia.ushmm.org/content/en/article/riga.

- The history of conversos (*Bnei Anusim*) is a fascinating one where DNA testing and family customs reveal a lineage that stretches to the Spanish Inquisition. More insight here: https://www.tabletmag.com/sections/news/articles/the-converso-comeback.

Thank you for reading *B is for Bowie*. **If you have any kind words about your reading experience, then I would be deeply indebted if you could share them on the site at which you purchased the book.** Keep your eyes peeled for *D is for dB*, coming soon. The lowercase d is intentional; can you guess what his weapon is?

If you didn't enjoy *B is for Bowie*, I appreciate you taking a chance on an unknown writer. Your time and money are important. May your next reading experience be better.

ABOUT THE AUTHOR

E.L. Snow is a Southerner living in the Northeast, who loves reading, reality television, and rosé wine. Feel free to contact her at ellysnowauthor@gmail.com if you have feedback or suggestions for future installments of ASSASSINZ.

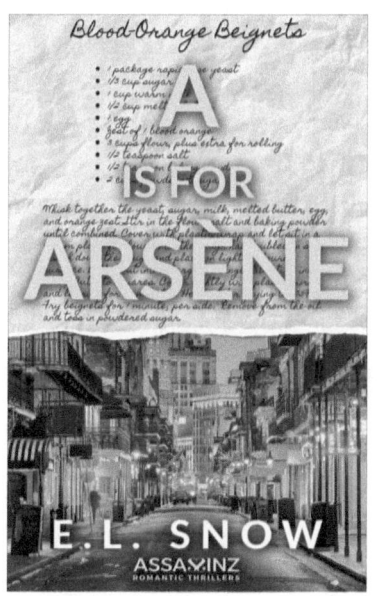

Coming soon

D is for dB